ALAN COLE DOESN'T DANCE

ALAN COLE DOESN'T DANCE

ERIC BELL

Katherine Tegen Books
An Imprint of HarperCollinsPublishers

Katherine Tegen Books is an imprint of HarperCollins Publishers.

Alan Cole Doesn't Dance
 For information address HarperCollins Children's Books, a division of HarperCollins Publishers, 195 Broadway, New York, NY 10007.
www.harpercollinschildrens.com

Library of Congress Cataloging-in-Publication Data

Names: Bell, Eric, 1985– author.
Title: Alan Cole doesn't dance / Eric Bell.
Other titles: Alan Cole does not dance
Description: First edition. | New York, NY : Katherine Tegen Books, an imprint of HarperCollinsPublishers, 2018. | Summary: As if it were not bad enough to be bullied for being gay while trying to navigate a budding relationship, Alan's father insists he take June Harrison to a school dance.
Identifiers: LCCN 2018013961 | ISBN 9780062567062 (hardback)
Subjects: | CYAC: Gays—Fiction. | Bullying—Fiction. | Friendship—Fiction. | Middle schools—Fiction. | Schools—Fiction. | Family problems—Fiction. | Brothers—Fiction. | Dance parties—Fiction. | BISAC: JUVENILE FICTION / Family / General (see also headings under Social Issues). | JUVENILE FICTION / Social Issues / Bullying.
Classification: LCC PZ7.1.B4515 Aj 2018 | DDC [Fic]—dc23 LC record available at https://lccn.loc.gov/2018013961

Typography by Aurora Parlagreco
18 19 20 21 22 CG/LSCH 10 9 8 7 6 5 4 3 2 1

First Edition

To Rachel Kobin and my fellow writers at the Philadelphia Writers Workshop, the birthplace of Alan Cole

ONE

A wise philosopher once said, "Personal change is like a slow, painful, heaving round of vomit. It's gross and embarrassing while it happens, but relieving and kind of refreshing when you're done." I think it's an ancient proverb.

Whether there's metaphorical puke or not—in my case I've spent more time blowing long hair out of my eyes than blowing chunks over a toilet—I realize now that the hardest thing about personal change is how the person you leave behind and the person you're on your way to becoming don't fully line up at first, like a shaky hand on paper. But that shaky hand gets steady eventually, and before you know it you're used to the new change. And that's that.

Except, of course, you're never done changing.

“Hey, Alan,” Zack interrupts my inner monologue with a chipper whisper. “Do you think the radioactive man-beasts come out of that little tube?”

I squint at the Mercury Nuclear Power Plant’s pressurized water reactor (at least that’s what the tour guide called it). “I don’t think they’d fit,” I whisper back.

“Radioactive man-beasts can stretch and contort their bodies into all kinds of shapes,” Zack says. “I bet if we asked Francine really nicely, she’d tell us the truth.”

I don’t think Francine, our tour guide, wants to answer Zack’s questions, let alone cart around a bunch of middle schoolers on a field trip. When Miss Richter said all the Accelerated School Placement Enrichment and Nourishment (ASPEN) classes, seventh graders through ninth graders (so that’s Saplings, Sprouts, and Shrubs, in ascending order—yep, you read that right), were taking a field trip to a nuclear plant, I thought it’d be more exciting than watching water rush around. Zack keeps insisting Francine is “hiding the deadly truths about nuclear power” due to government conspiracies.

“Hush,” Madison whispers, putting a finger to his mouth. “You’re missing all the important facts.”

“Who can tell me the difference between nuclear fission and nuclear fusion?” Francine asks.

Madison’s hand shoots into the air. “Nuclear fission

involves the splitting of atoms, whereas nuclear fusion involves the joining of atoms," he recites.

"That's right," Francine says.

"Fatison could use some splitting of his atoms, huh?" an eighth-grade (I try not to use the plant terminology if I can help it, because I have some measure of self-respect) girl whispers, leading to some nearby snickering.

"Hmph." Madison crosses his arms but doesn't say anything in response.

As we move away from the pressurized water reactor, I say to Madison, "I bet they're jealous. They probably didn't know what nuclear fission was before—"

Someone bumps into me, hard from behind, knocking me off balance. Zack reaches out to steady me. "Hey!" he yelps.

"Oh sorry," a ninth-grade guy says. "Didn't see you there, Galan."

The guy walks away without a teacher noticing. Madison sighs. "At least *Fatison* is on its way out. I worry there's a lot more mileage they'll be getting from *Galan*."

"The name doesn't even make sense," Zack says. "It sounds like a prescription drug."

"Gay Alan," Madison mutters.

Zack's eyes get wide. "Ohhhhh. I get it now. Wouldn't it be *Gaylan* then? You should petition to change the name. If they're going to make fun of you, they should at least *try*. Right?"

My reputation as the guy who likes other guys came about a month ago, at the end of my brother Nathan's game of Cole vs. Cole, or CvC. Nathan, who'd practically made a full-time job out of turning my life into a waking nightmare, threatened to out me to all of Evergreen Middle School if I lost the game. And even though I won, I still came out because I wanted to stop being afraid of my brother, and of the rest of the world. Now I'm getting to know a loud minority of kids who think it's funny to call me *Galan*, who like to taunt and shove me when the teachers aren't looking. It's like I've traded in one gigantic bully for a bunch of smaller ones.

Right now my attention is focused on Nathan, two years my senior, hovering within earshot. He watches me, I guess to make sure I'm not hurt, even though he could've intervened but didn't. Marcellus Mitchell, his best friend, whispers something in his ear, and Nathan makes this jerky half-step in my direction, but then he and Marcellus leave us behind.

"It's been a month," Zack says as we catch up with the rest of the group. "I'm surprised he hasn't stood up for you."

"Not once," I say.

"Hmph," Madison scoffs. "If you want my honest

opinion, I'm not surprised. He tortured you for years. Someone with such a cruel streak isn't going to change on a dime." He frowns. "Or ever."

After I won CvC, I made Nathan swear off his dark ways. I guess I didn't specify he had to actively be a good person though. He's barely said one word to me this past month, which is, granted, a huge improvement over the past twelve years of our relationship. But I was hoping for a normal big brother. One who sticks up for his little bro if his little bro runs into homophobia every day.

The giant clump of kids congregates around what looks like a gift shop. "We're offering a special twenty-five percent student discount on Mercury Power Plant merchandise," Francine says like she's reading off a teleprompter.

"Do you have T-shirts?" Rudy Brighton, my seventh-grade classmate, asks.

"We've got a few," Francine says.

Rudy pumps his fist into the air and leads the way into the gift shop.

Instead of walking into the incredibly fascinating gift shop, Miss Richter, my favorite teacher, snaps her fingers. "None of that," she says to someone I can't see. I crane my neck and—

Ugh.

Connor Garcia—the straight guy I'm still, despite

knowing it'll never work out between us, crushing on—is laughing, flashing his big smile at Sheila Carter. She gets to see a lot of his big smile lately because Connor and Sheila are officially a *couple*. Officially *dating*. Officially getting into plenty of PDA *every single day*, which is totally gross and I'm not jealous at all. Nope. Why would you get that idea?

I force my eye to stop twitching.

"Alan Cole," a voice from behind me barks, startling me so much my skeleton practically jumps out of my skin.

"Hi," I say in between deep breaths.

Talia MacDonald, our class president, doesn't look happy. Then again, Talia hasn't looked happy much lately. Maybe the stress of running an entire grade is getting to her. She's pitched three million ideas to Principal Dorset for "ways to improve the middle school experience," and he's only approved one of them. And I know that one idea is why she wants to talk to me.

"You know why I want to talk to you," she says. (What did I tell you?)

I nod. "Because there's too many people to fit into the gift shop."

Talia puts her hands on her hips. "This isn't a laughing matter. I tried to launch 'Where Do We Come From?' a month ago, and I've only had three participants. I keep waiting for an Alan Cole masterpiece to christen the display, but thus far you've given me absolutely squat."

She's right. And it burns. Last month I shared with Talia (and Zack and Madison) the idea for my cretpoj, the painting that became my self-portrait. That inspired Talia's big project about understanding each other. That's what I want to do with my cretpoj: change the world. It would make sense for me to contribute something that shows where I came from. Who I am. What I believe in. But . . .

"It's not done," I say. "I'll let you know when it is."

"You keep saying that," Talia says, shaking her head. "I'm starting to think you don't want anyone to see your . . . crunkpot, was it?"

"Cretpoj."

"Whatever it is, I want it. If I have to grab that sketchbook of yours and squeeze it out with my bare hands, I will. Don't test me!" She stomps off toward the crowded gift shop.

I breathe easier. My hands pat my sketchbook reflexively, nestled in my backpack. The truth is . . . my cretpoj is done. It's been done for three weeks. I spent hours cooped up in my room with a tiny mirror and my paints, making the most whiplashing, neck-cracking, earthquake-inducing, pressurized-water-reacting painting known to humanity. It's going to make the whole world throw up.

I have shown it to absolutely no one.

I love to paint. I live to paint. If art was breathing, I'd cry watercolors. Zack and Madison keep asking me about it. Talia keeps asking me about it. The world is waiting for me to unveil it. Why can't I even take it out of my sketchbook?

When I think about my cretpoj just sitting in my sketchbook turning yellow, it makes me sick. To make things even worse, I haven't painted anything at all since I finished it. No people, no puppies, no plants. Not even stick figures. For all the good I've done over the past month, it all starts to unravel whenever I think about the fact that I'm sitting on my purpose in life, hands firmly squashed under my butt, losing muscle memory, turning to dust. What's the problem? What am I afraid of?

"You okay?" Zack asks as the classes awkwardly shovel themselves into the gift shop. He's already changed into an "I <3 My Power Plant" T-shirt.

"I'm fine," I say. If I keep telling myself that, I will be.

Madison puffs out his chest. He clutches a mug with a nuclear reactor design that says "The Fission Commission." "Well, gentlemen, I'd say this field trip was a fantastic success. We learned so much about nuclear power and how safe and efficient it is."

"We didn't learn about the radioactive man-beasts

though," Zack says. "Do you think this shirt brings out the color in my hair?"

"You don't need any help drawing attention to your hair," Madison says.

Zack picks at a loose strand of his bird's nest of a hairstyle, flopping in between his eyebrows. "I guess not. Hey, slumber party this weekend?"

I perk up. "That'd be great."

"For the last time, call them *sleepovers*," Madison groans. "Much more mature. I'll need to check with my parents, but it should be fine."

Zack smiles. "Best friends. Now and forever."

We all bump fists, extending and touching our thumbs.

I'll let you in on a little secret—sometimes I think I haven't changed enough yet. Sometimes I look at my friends, so brave and strong, and I see in myself something else. Sometimes I look at my cretpoj, and I don't see the Alan of tomorrow. I see the Alan of yesterday, a yesterday I hoped I'd left behind. That's the thing about change: it's hard—but hopefully it's doable too. So I keep changing. I keep struggling. And maybe eventually, maybe someday, my shaky hands will make a masterpiece.

TWO

The next day, after I get off bus 19, I walk past the community board by the school entrance and overhear some kids talking about the upcoming Winter Dance, a shared effort between Evergreen and our rival, Broadleaf Middle School. It's not for another few weeks and already people are falling over themselves to get dates. I never got the appeal of dances—you jerk your body around like you're having muscle spasms while wearing uncomfortable clothes inside a stuffy room packed full of other people having muscle spasms, and you try not to look like an utter disaster, which is impossible due to, once again, looking like you're having muscle spasms. Besides, I don't dance. (And the guy I'd want to go with already has a *girlfriend*.)

The flyer for the dance reads, "Winter Dance!" surrounded by clip art snowflakes. But something else is pinned to the board. Something that wasn't there yesterday:

Calling all artists!
The Gladstone Art Academy is taking applications for our winter term. Six weekends of intensive art instruction and exploration.
Visit gladstoneartacademy.org for details and applications.

My mouth hangs open so wide a bird could fly inside. The Gladstone Art Academy is based in Philadelphia, about forty-five minutes from Petal Fields. It's got an incredible reputation for its classes, held every three years, for aspiring artists between the ages of twelve and eighteen. Victoria Gladstone, the woman who runs it, has work displayed in prominent museums. Not to mention all the prodigies she's tutored—there's Chance Palmer, the teenage sculpture genius (who's also really cute—not that I've noticed), and Yolanda Byron, who works in glass and pottery *and* textiles, and so many other people who are big in the local art scene. I could be Victoria Gladstone's next artistic prodigy. And it could help me get over my artist's block! That would be an astronomical experience. I hope no one slips in all the drool I'm leaking over the floor.

But it's an astronomical experience I don't have the rocket ship for. If I can't even show my cretpoj to my friends, how could I show a class full of strangers, who are probably all way better artists than me? Plus I haven't done *any* post-cretpoj art at all. On top of that, the academy is *really* selective. Oh well. Nice knowing you for five seconds, dream.

"What are you staring at?" Madison comes up behind me. "You're not joining the Percussion Club, are you? Their flyer says they're 'drumming up interest.' Would you really want to be in a club like that?"

"Nothing," I say.

Madison crosses his arms. "You're a terrible liar. Let's see . . . cheerleading, choir, community service . . . Oh ho, what's this?"

"See you in homeroom," I say, walking away.

He catches up with me quickly. "An art academy would be perfect for you."

"No, it wouldn't," I say.

"Are you still upset about not showing anyone your crackpaunch?"

"Cretpoj."

"So you're shy about it. Think of all the opportunities

the academy could bring. Think of all the connections you could make! The Philadelphia art world is vibrant, you know. I say go for it."

"Thanks for the advice," I say.

Madison shakes his head. "Alan, I thought you were braver than this."

I stop walking.

"The Alan I know wouldn't let a little thing like art shyness stop him from pursuing his dreams. He would march forward with confidence and wouldn't take no for an answer."

I look up at Madison. "I'll leave a message on his voicemail, and I'll let you know when he gets back to me."

Madison frowns at first. Then he realizes I'm joking, and he smiles. "Atta boy."

We walk into homeroom. My friend is right. What am I afraid of? I should do it. I should seize the life-changing opportunity. I should stand in the sun and bask in its rays.

I should figure out who this kid sitting in my desk is.

Huh?

There's a kid sitting in my desk. He's flipping through a book. His notebook and pencil and papers sit on top of his—*my*—desk. I've never seen him before, but he's already made himself at home.

Madison shrugs at me. I walk over to my desk. "Um, excuse me."

The kid doesn't look up, still intently reading his book.

"Excuse me," I say a little louder. "You're, uh, you're in my—"

"Do you mind?" he asks. "I'm near the end of this chapter." He turns the page.

My mouth flops open again. This time you could fit a turtle inside. "That's my desk," I say. "You're in my desk."

He holds up a finger.

Most of the room has already filed inside. Madison has taken his seat across the room from my desk. *My desk.* Not this kid's. Mine!

Miss Richter isn't here yet, so I can't go to her. A few of the other students keep eyeing this new kid, probably wondering who he is, where he came from, and why he's *sitting in my desk.*

"Alan Cole, sit down," Talia says. "You're blocking the whiteboard."

"I can't," I grit through my teeth. "He's in my seat."

"Ask him to leave," Talia says. "New kid! With the book!"

He finishes popping a bookmark inside his book and puts it away.

"You're in someone else's seat," Talia continues. "As your class president, I'm advising you to find another desk." She says to me, "You are not assertive at all, do you know that?"

"I feel like sitting here today," he says.

A vein in my forehead feels like it's about to burst. "Just sit somewhere else. That's. My. Desk!"

Miss Richter walks in, followed by Zack, who takes the seat next to mine. He doesn't look up and says to the desk thief, "Hi, Alan. Did you fill out the discussion questions for English? Do you think Mrs. Ront is going to agree with me that *Hatchet* is actually about ballet? I mean, you see it, right?"

"Alan, why aren't you sitting down?" Miss Richter asks.

I take a deep breath. "*Hesinmydesk.*"

My homeroom teacher looks down the room and sees the desk snatcher. "Ah, you must be our new student. Why don't you pull up a desk from the back and put it somewhere in the square? You're in another student's seat right now."

The kid, now free from book distractions, gives me the dirtiest glare imaginable, dipped in arsenic and hemlock and mud. He gathers up his stuff, and I fly into my desk, convinced that if I don't, he'll steal it from me again. But then I hear the unmistakable noise of a desk screeching on linoleum, and lo and behold, the desk bandit is shrieking his desk right next to mine, in between me and Zack. We extend the three-sided square so there's room for his desk, and there is much screeching and shrieking and unpleasant noise, and the whole experience is enough to jar me out of any good mood I might have been in from Madison's pep talk.

"Thank you," Miss Richter says. "Would you like to introduce yourself? Or should I do it?"

"It's fine," the desk bandit says. He takes the time to reorganize his desk—notebook, pencil, what looks like a schedule printout, various papers of various colors—before saying another word. Finally, after what has to be a full minute, he says, "My name is Odin Thompson. I'm ready to kick ass."

A few snickers bounce about the room. On the other side of me, Connor smiles. "Rock on, man."

"Thank you, Odin," Miss Richter says. "In the future, let's try to put the PG in PG-13, okay?"

"Hang on," Rudy says. "Did you say your name was Odin? Like Thor's dad? That Odin?"

"Yeah," Odin says, like he's waiting for Rudy to challenge his right to his name.

Rudy grins. "That is *so cool.*"

Across the square, Madison's arms are firmly crossed over his chest. Zack stares curiously at his new neighbor, like Odin is juggling chain saws while riding a unicycle. And I'm sitting here, hoping this Norse god isn't going to keep being as much of a royal pain as he's been so far.

When the bell rings for first period, Odin's stuff is all packed up and ready to go. And you know what? I want to be the bigger person. The Alan I know marches forward with confidence. And compassion. Besides, Lord knows I've forgiven people for worse. "Hi," I say to him. "I think we got off on the wrong foot. If you want a hand figuring out Evergreen, let me know. It can be really confusing sometimes."

Odin frowns. "What makes you think I need your help?"

"Uh, just that this school is big, and I've been here two months, and this is, uh, your first day—"

"I can handle myself. You saying I can't?"

"No. I was—"

"Tell you what. You let me figure out school by myself, and I'll leave you alone. We got a deal?"

Sweat starts prickling my back. "Uh, I, I was—"

"We got a deal, String Bean?"

I take a deep breath. "Sure."

He walks past me out the door. Zack and Madison both give me looks of complete confusion, maybe because he called me *String Bean* when he's as tall and skinny as I am. Or because he was a total jerk to me for no reason.

Ugh.

"Some people are beyond help," Madison says as he leaves. "You tried. Now it's best to ignore him."

Zack shakes his head as he follows me to my swimming class (even though his first period isn't even close to the pool). "Nobody's beyond help. Once he sees how great a guy you are, he'll want to be your friend for sure."

Except I don't want him to be my friend. I'd be happier if he stayed out of my desk, didn't give me nicknames (I have enough of those), and didn't treat me like I was gum in his hair. In fact, it'd be great if he left me alone entirely. I don't need any more friends, but even more than that, I definitely don't need any more enemies.

THREE

Swimming class is still an ordeal. Don't get me wrong—I don't mind the actual swimming anymore. Passing the test a month ago is one of my proudest accomplishments. Even though it's taken me some time to learn the exercises the rest of the class does, it's not the swimming that's the problem.

The reason that swimming still sucks is one of my fellow swimmers.

I stare up at the lights in the locker room, careful not to make eye contact with anyone. That'd be the loaded gun full of Alan-caliber bullets. I usually ignore everyone else in the locker room until they all head to the pool, and I do the same on the way back in until we're all changed. It's safer this way.

Today, however, Ron McCaughlin walks into the

locker room with a face that screams pissed off. When I came out, Connor said he'd protect me from his buddy Ron, who hates gay people like vampires hate sun, so Ron largely kept his distance for a little while. But Connor's barely paid me any mind ever since he started dating Sheila, which means Ron's moved closer and closer to his prey, preparing to serve up an Alan-kabob when no one's looking. Nothing's happened. Yet.

So when Ron marches into the locker room and barks, "Don't look at me," my nerves tingle. Is today the day? Is this Ron's breaking point, the day he unloads all his anti-gay rage out on me?

"I wasn't," I say.

He sneers. "You calling me a liar?"

There are lots of things I could call Ron, but none of them are printable. I go back to changing, praying he'll go away soon.

No such luck. "I said, you calling me a liar, homo?"

Now the whole locker room hears us. I gulp. "No."

"Then you were looking at me."

"I wasn't—"

"So I'm a liar. Can't make up your mind, huh, Galan? Maybe I'll make it up for you."

I want to tell Ron what he said doesn't make sense—making up my mind isn't really a threat—but more than that, I want to stop sweating, and even more than *that*,

I want Ron to go away. But Ron's like a speeding truck without brakes: the only way to stop it is to crash it.

So I take a deep breath and I say, "You're not my type."

He squints. "Huh?"

I look him dead in the eye. "You're not my type. Sorry." (Except I'm not sorry, because it's not my fault. But all good burns end with "sorry." It's a fact.)

Ron doesn't know how to process this. "I'm not your—" Then he screams, "Ewww!"

"Yeah, Ron," Jamal Lawrence says, standing at the locker next to me. "He likes smart guys." That comment provokes a chorus of echoing laughs all through the locker room.

Ron is losing all his steam. His truck smashes into a tree and catches fire. "You're sick," he spits at me. He walks out toward the pool.

I stop holding my breath.

I don't regain my composure until everyone is out of the locker room except me. Me and one other guy.

"That was stupid," Marcellus Mitchell says from behind me in his even, deep bass voice.

"He could have beaten me up," I say.

Nathan's best friend and I walk out to the pool together. "He still could," Marcellus says. "All you're doing is giving him ammo."

"I can't sit back and do nothing," I say quietly.

Marcellus considers me for a long moment. "I guess you can't."

As Coach Streit's student lifeguard and remedial swim coach, Marcellus oversaw my progress—or lack thereof, thanks to him—when it came to learning how to swim. Showing up one day, ready to pass the test after I trained in secret with Madison, blindsided him. Ever since then, he talks to me occasionally—which is more than Nathan has done—and sometimes even gives me advice, but never when anyone else is around.

I make my way to the stands overlooking the pool. Ron is telling a joke to a group of girls, and Marcellus is doing neck stretches, and Coach Streit is talking to—

Oh, *come on*.

"Let me get this straight," the coach says, looking down at the little paper in her hands. "You have a—"

"Chlorine allergy, yeah," Odin says. "So I can't take swimming."

"A chlorine allergy."

"That's what the note says."

Coach Streit sighs. "Well, once we call this doctor and verify your . . . allergy, we'll get you set up with a different gym program. In the meantime, have a seat in the stands and watch."

Odin hoists his backpack over his shoulders, sits in

the highest rung of the bleachers, pulls out his book, and starts reading. He doesn't seem to notice me.

What I've learned about the new kid:

Fact #1: He knows how to forge doctor's notes.

Fact #2: He doesn't know how to swim.

Chlorine allergy. Right.

When I walk home to 16 Werther Steet from the bus stop, Mom is sitting in the kitchen, reading a book. She walks over and gives me a hug and a kiss. She's given me hugs and kisses every day for the past month, often multiple times a day. After eight years of being as detached from her family as the planet Neptune and letting Dad rule the roost like a diamond-encrusted chicken, Mom's been making up for lost time, and I'm sure not complaining.

I've gone over my sales pitch a dozen times. Here goes nothing. "Mom, have you ever heard of the Gladstone Art Academy?"

"I don't think so," she says.

"It's this intensive six-week-long art program they run in the city. They're taking applications for it now. I think it'd be a great opportunity for me to be around other artists, and Victoria Gladstone is a, uh, really successful artist herself, and she's tutored lots of other artists who went on to be famous. I could learn—I could learn things no one in Petal Fields could teach me. And, uh, the classes are only offered every three years because of Victoria Gladstone's travel schedule. This would be one of the only times I can go. So can I go?"

Mom smiles. "That would be great. How much is it?"

"A thousand dollars," I murmur.

"Sorry, I didn't hear you. What did you say?"

"It's a thousand bucks."

Her smile falters. "For six weeks? That's a lot of money . . ."

"It's six weekends, really," I mumble. I knew it wouldn't work. I squeeze my hands tight.

But Mom's not done. "I think it sounds great," she says. She gives me another kiss on the cheek. "I can't promise anything, but I'll see what I can do."

That's the best I'm getting from her. And if I can't get Mom on board this sinking ship, Dad's certainly not going to plug the leak. I know money's been tighter than usual lately. While Dad hopes for that always-out-of-reach promotion, Mom's gotten a few extra hours helping our church. She loves to cook, but lately we've had a few frozen entrees and buckets of KFC for dinner. And instead of buying me new winter clothes, Mom and Dad gave me some of Nathan's greatest hits, even though they're more than a little small on me.

Later, at the dinner table, the smells of Italian sausage

and tomato basil sauce fill the house. Dad carefully and deliberately twirls his linguine around his fork, skewering his sausage without getting a single speck anywhere. Across the table Nathan eats in silence, staring at his plate. After we all finish our second helpings, I look at Mom, who nods. "Dad," I say.

Dad looks at me.

I try keeping my voice steady. Dad's traditionally been about as kind and understanding as a wooden plank with jagged nails poking out of it. Like Mom, he's been trying to change lately, so he hasn't been as harsh as he's always been, but he's still not a cuddly bunny either. "I was wondering if I could apply to the Gladstone Art Academy."

"The Gladstone What Academy?"

"Art. Gladstone Art Academy." This is a problem. He's already zoomed in on the art part. An image of our fireplace burning a sketchbook, permanently seared across my brain, lunges forward, but I shove it back down.

Dad leans forward slowly. "Don't you do enough art in school? At home? Why do we need to send you somewhere?"

"It's a great opportunity to be around other artists. And there are tons of success stories, and the woman who runs it is—"

"How much?"

I don't say anything. Mom watches both of us, taking deep breaths.

Dad laughs. "Girls don't like guys who do art. Lord knows you need all the help you can get."

Now I turn bright red. This whole month, ever since CvC ended, I haven't told him. Or Mom. I get so angry when I think about it. Everyone at school knows. Why can't they? I think about how things are different now . . . but not different enough. Maybe they'll never be enough.

"We can't afford it," Dad says. "Money's tight. You'll have to keep painting at home instead."

I look down at my plate, losing myself in the sauce.

"Jimmy." At the other end of the table, Mom looks right at Dad. "He's going to this."

Dad's face is blank.

"Alan never asks for anything," Mom continues. "Never. This is all he wants. We owe it to him."

"I'm not—"

"*You* owe it to him."

Dad matches Mom's steely gaze, and Mom, despite her newfound confidence, looks down at the table for a few seconds. Nathan picks at his pasta. My heart feels like it's running laps around the rest of my body. "There's, uh, a chance I won't get in," I say, stupidly. "I could apply and, uh, if I get in, then we can talk about it. . . . "

"How much?" Dad asks.

"We can afford it," Mom says, steadying herself. "With enough saving, we can afford it."

Dad takes a few big gulps of water. He looks me over. "This is really what you want to do?"

I nod.

He closes his eyes and massages his temples. "Then you can do it."

The weight gets sucked off my back and I can breathe again. He said it! He really said it! You heard him, right?

Mom smiles warmly. She reaches across the table and squeezes Dad's hand. Dad looks at her, shock written over his face, and after a few seconds he slides his thumb over her knuckles.

Then he pulls away. "I wasn't finished. You can do it . . . if you do something for me."

Uh-oh.

"You remember Mr. Harrison's daughter?"

June. A patch of poison ivy in the rose garden of life. When I was dragged to Dad's company dinner last month, June Harrison got me into serious trouble, and Dad wound up . . . doing something really bad to my sketchbook. Involving the fireplace. Never trust a girl who carries roadkill around in her purse.

"Of course you do," Dad continues without waiting for

me to respond. "Mr. Harrison tells me there's a dance coming up at your school."

I blink, not understanding. Nathan finally comes to life, practically choking on his water.

"I want you to go with June," Dad says.

My heart gets impaled with a thousand needles. "With June? To—to the dance?"

"It would smooth things over," Dad continues. "I might still be able to get that promotion if you behave and don't do anything stupid. That'll really help the family out. Play your cards, and you might even get to date her, which would be great."

"She goes to Broadleaf, not Evergreen," I sputter, brain scraping out any excuses it can find.

"That won't be a problem," Dad replies. "The dance is for both schools. I checked."

I can't believe this. "I'm not going with June. I can't. I won't."

"You will if you want to go to this art academy," Dad says. "*You* owe it to *me* for that disastrous company dinner. Understand?"

I gulp and bow my head. Overshot that one.

"Jimmy," Mom says, a note of warning crackling in her voice.

Dad sighs, looking like he's fraying at the edges. "It would be very good for me if you did this."

Going to the dance is bad enough. Going with *June* is torture. If this is the only way I can apply to Gladstone though . . . what choice do I have? I catch Nathan staring at me from across the table; when I make eye contact, he looks down.

"Can I think about it?" I ask.

Dad grunts. "Think fast." He stands up and walks to the garage, signaling that dinner is officially over. Nathan follows suit, retreating to his room, ever the non-presence.

This could've been a lot worse, but it could've been a heck of a lot better too. How can I go to the dance with a girl like June? How can I go to the dance with a *girl*? How can I go to the dance *at all*?

I help Mom clear the table and do the dishes. As she rinses the colander, I say, "Thanks."

She puts a finger on my lips, kisses my cheek, and goes back to washing.

Like I said—making up for lost time. But I'll take it.

FOUR

"Slumber! Party! Slumber! Party! Slumber! Party! Slumber—"

"We get it," Madison sighs at Zack, who's bouncing around his tiny bedroom, jumping up and down on his bed, and dancing some odd combination of popping, locking, and can-canning. Once Zack grabs his pillow and feeds his turtle, Oprah, we migrate back to the living room, where I've still got half a slice of pizza to conquer.

"Okay, I'm going to bed," Ms. Kimble says. "Remember: not too loud. I know thumping and screaming is what twelve-year-old boys do, but the Chens downstairs don't appreciate it. So please refrain yourselves from too much thumpage and screamage."

"Yes, ma'am," Madison says. "There will be no thumping or screaming. I'll make sure of it."

Ms. Kimble isn't what you might expect from a woman who birthed Zack. She's shockingly normal—no paper clip earrings or glow-in-the-dark pajamas (Zack, as you might imagine, has both). She is, however, exceptionally cool, which is why we always have sleepovers at the Kimbles' apartment despite me and Madison both living in much larger houses.

Zack runs over and gives his mom a hug. "Night, Mom," he says. "Love you."

"Love you too," she says.

"Good night, Ms. Kimble," I say.

"Sleep well," she says, closing her bedroom door.

Madison shakes his head. "It always shocks me to hear you tell your mother you love her. I don't remember the last time my parents said that to me."

"Yeah, same here," I say, chewing on my pizza slice.

"We say it every day," Zack says. "That's how it's always been."

"I'm sure it's healthier than what we do," Madison scoffs. "Did you know my mother stood in the treadmill room with me for an hour today, and she wouldn't leave until I ran three miles? Three miles! If you want my honest opinion, man wasn't meant to run for three miles."

Madison's parents are still trying to get him to lose a bunch of weight. He told them if he was going to lose weight he wanted it to be on his own terms, to get in shape, not for cosmetic reasons (even though he's still insecure about the whole *Fatison* thing). They laughed at him and said that was proof he wasn't ready to make important decisions on his own. Now they're shipping him off to Helen's Crest Health and Fitness Club all throughout the week until he loses fifteen pounds. I go with him whenever I can for moral support.

"You could always go back to the pool," I say.

"She won't let me unless you're there. She trusts you to keep me in line. That's better than trusting her own son, I suppose." Madison carves at his pizza with a plastic knife and fork so hard the paper plate gets ripped.

Zack rolls up all the cheese on his pizza slice and chews on it like a Twizzler. "I'd come with you, but the only exercise I know how to do is jumping jacks. Unless you want me to bark instructions at you with a bullhorn while you run." He pauses. "Nah. I could never yell at you."

"That's not the worst of it," Madison says. "They're threatening to make me work with a personal trainer. Those people are like drill instructors! Can you believe this? They're going to work me so ragged I'll barely be able to move. And they keep restricting my diet. This pizza is the only real food I've had all week."

Zack finishes swallowing his rolled-up cheese. "It sounds like they're worried about you."

"Worried?" Madison asks. "Why would they be worried? Because I'm *fat*?"

I start, "You're not—"

"Of course I am. And I was okay with that. Mostly. It would be nice to lose a few pounds to get in better shape. But my parents aren't concerned about my health. They want me to lose weight so girls will like me. So I won't be unpopular. It's not going to make a difference." He stabs his pizza slice with his plastic fork so ferociously one of the prongs snaps off.

Suddenly Zack gasps so cartoonishly, he starts choking. "We need to get you a date for the dance!"

Sweat starts to prickle on my back. I was putting off mentioning the June situation, but it looks like it's creeping up from the dank underbelly of existence, infecting everything with toxic waste.

Madison examines his broken fork. "Don't make fun of me."

"I'm serious!" Zack yells. "If we can get you a date to the dance, it'll prove to your parents you don't need to be skinny for girls to like you. Then maybe they'd leave you alone. Right?"

"I don't want to go to the dance."

"Why not? It could be fun. Alan's going, right?"

"Uh," I stammer, "I-I-I'm not sure."

"And I don't want a date, or a girlfriend, or anything

like that," Madison grumbles. "I'm not interested."

Zack rips off his crust and bites huge chunks off it. "She wouldn't even have to go out with you. If she's even a little interested, that could be enough."

Madison stands up to throw out his fork. "Fine. Find me a girl who's actually interested in me, and we'll take it from there. But if you can't find me someone suitable by the dance, you're going to drop it forever. Understood?"

Zack salutes Madison. "You got it. This'll be fun! Matchmaking can't be too hard."

"And what about you?" Madison asks Zack, washing his hands. "Are you going to go as a solo act? Or are you staying home?"

"Neither," Zack says with a smile. "I know who I'm asking: Meredith Wood."

Madison raises both eyebrows. "But Meredith Wood is a very popular Sapling."

"Yeah," I say. "I didn't think you'd go for a popular girl."

"She's popular, but that's not why I love her," Zack says. He holds his hands up to his heart. "I love her because she's sweet and kind and friendly and happy and she has a little lisp on *s* words and she has a puppy and she has hazel eyes *like me* and when we get married we'll have our ceremony on the beach and live in a lighthouse and direct oncoming boat traffic. Meredith Wood is my soul mate."

"Zack," I say very patiently, "you said the same thing about Penny." Zack had a massive crush on Penny Schmidt, who said some nasty things about him—to his face.

Zack keeps smiling. "That was different. Penny wasn't my soul mate. Meredith is. I can't wait to ask her to the dance." He stops and thinks about something. "My mom has a boyfriend."

"Whoa," I say. "You didn't tell us that."

"Goodness, that's big news," Madison says. "Is this her first boyfriend since your father . . ."

"Yeah," Zack says. "Since Dad died. He seems okay, I guess."

"You don't sound too excited," Madison says.

Zack shrugs. "I don't know. It's not important. I don't even know why I brought him up. Let's talk about the dance some more. I can't wait to show Meredith the Zack Shuffle." He stands up and does this horrific gyration that looks like he's being electrocuted and drowned at the same time.

Now, I know Zack Kimble, and Zack does and does not want to talk about his mom's new boyfriend at the same time. That means something's up. But I don't press the issue. Besides, I have something to share too. "Guys," I say, "I need to tell you something."

"Ooh, do you have a guy you're going with?" Zack asks, taking big bites from his now cheeseless and crustless pizza. "Do you have a secret admirer who writes you love letters?"

I tell them about Dad's ultimatum: go with June or don't go to Gladstone. "Huh," Madison says. "That's . . . something all right."

"Yeah," Zack says. He gathers together all the plates and napkins and tosses them in the trash. "He must've been pretty disappointed when you said no."

I don't say anything.

Zack returns to the table. "I bet your dad didn't even see it coming. You really showed him."

Madison's eyes flicker back and forth between us.

I sigh. "I didn't say no."

Zack's eyes bulge out. "You—you what?"

"I didn't say yes either, though. I said I had to think about it."

Zack looks confused. Even more than usual. "What's there to think about? You don't like girls. You can't go as June's date."

"Why not?" Madison pipes up. "It's not as if they're

getting married. Friends go to dances together all the time."

"Yeah," I say. "Except my dad was pretty clear it was a date."

"Alan!" Zack says, sounding unusually forceful. "What happened to being yourself?"

"I don't know," I say. "It's only one dance. I'd do anything to go to this academy. The opportunities I'd get would be amazing. And it's only once every three years. I have to go."

Zack sputters like he's a song that's stuck on a beat. "Yeah, but, but, but you're going against who you are. How can you do that?"

Now I frown. "There's more to me than being *gay*, you know."

I stop and lose all my forward momentum once I realize this is the first time I've ever referred to myself as . . . gay, either out loud or even in my head. Like someone scratched a needle, the room stops, and I let myself soak in the word, see how it sounds, feels, tastes.

It fits.

I'd always kept open the back door in my brain that maybe there'd be a girl someday I'd fall for, but with this new puzzle piece sliding into place, that possibility seems to slip farther and farther away.

And I'm . . . okay with that. I'm fine being . . . gay.

Zack stares at me. "If I find you a guy to go to the dance with, will you go with him instead of June?"

Back to reality. I'm not used to Zack being unsupportive. This whole conversation has thrown me off. "I don't know what I'm doing yet. Okay?"

"Zack, please," Madison says. "Alan's got to figure this out himself and you're not helping. Just because he wants to try out girls for a bit isn't any reason to criticize him."

Great. Zero for two. "That's *not* what I'm doing," I say. "I don't like girls."

"Exactly!" Zack cries.

"But he should still try them out," Madison says with a nod of his head. "You know, in case. It's very logical."

"No, it's *not*," I say, my voice rising. "Do you think it's 'very logical' for you to think about dating guys? You know, in case?"

Madison frowns. "There's no need to get testy. I'm supporting your decision."

"No, you're not!" I yell. "Neither of you get it!"

"Watch the screamage!" Madison yells.

Zack puts his hands up. "Why don't we drop it? Let's play some *Mario Kart*. Have some fun. This is a slumber party and we're supposed to have fun. Right?"

"It's a sleepover, *thank you*," Madison grumbles.

But whatever you want to call it—*sleepover, slumber party, up-all-night hang-out-a-thon*—we do not have fun. The *Mario Kart* races quickly turn brutal, with Madison loudly grumbling about how me and Zack are cheating, and Zack trying extra hard to smooth things over by letting me and Madison win all the races (which only pisses Madison off even more), and me taking out my frustrations on both my friends by going out of my way to attack them every single time. After a few rounds, we all, by some unspoken agreement, decide to go to bed, even though it is well before the maximum bedtime requirement for a slumber party.

Of course, I can't sleep. And judging by how Madison isn't snoring and Zack keeps tossing and turning, neither can they.

I lie in my sleeping bag, rolled over onto my side, clenching and unclenching my fists. If anyone in the world understood the June situation, it would have—should have—been my friends. But they don't get it. And if they don't get it, who will?

They see me as Alan the Gay Kid. Not Alan the Artist Who's Also a Gay Kid. Maybe it's my own fault—if I could only show them my cretpoj, maybe then they'd see how much art means to me. But I can't, and they don't, and here we are, sitting in our sleeping bags, pretending to be asleep so we don't have to talk to each other.

My dad doesn't know who I am, and I don't think he would even if I showed him my cretpoj. And I guess even the people who matter, the ones sharing this tiny living room with me tonight, don't know everything about me either.

FIVE

I don't look forward to Monday. I couldn't go home fast enough on Sunday morning—which is a post-sleepover sentence I never thought I'd hear myself say—and the promise of a dreary Monday where I'm mad at my friends does not fill me with enthusiasm. The Monday bus ride overlooks a gloomy November morning, passing by plenty of leafless, stick-figure trees and a fog that won't quit. My bones have those achy, tired vibrations you get with damp, chilly days.

When I walk into homeroom, I'm at least pleased to see that Odin is not sitting in my desk. Breathing a little easier, I take my seat next to him while everyone else filters in. It looks like Odin's not reading today. He's—

Is he *sketching*?

I crane my neck. Yep, he's sketching on a piece of unlined paper. It looks like an elaborate drawing of a guy fighting a dragon, in a very expressive, anime style. I get lost in his technique for a few moments before he says, "Like what you see?"

I nod, then I realize he isn't looking at me. "It's cool."

"Well, make your own," he grumbles. "I don't do commissions."

"I've got my own, actually," I say. "I paint."

Odin stops sketching. He points to his denim jacket, which has several elaborate, painted designs all over the sleeves. "Bet you can't do this. Or this."

"It's not a competition, geez," I say. "Your stuff looks cool. I didn't realize that was a crime."

"Whatever, Coleslaw," he grumbles. He goes back to work.

I don't think I heard him right. "Did you call me *Coleslaw*?"

He doesn't react, so lost in adding in the dragon's scales. He's a quick worker, and on top of that he doesn't skimp on the details. I guess that's why he needs to focus. Also, Friday I was *String Bean*, today I'm *Coleslaw*. What's next? *Potato Salad*?

Eh. Beats *Galan* any day of the week. Even if this guy is still exasperating.

Zack gives me a hesitant smile when he walks in, but

I don't return it. Madison at least has the courtesy to not look at me on the way to his desk.

"Tickets for the Winter Dance will go on sale today during your lunch periods," Principal Dorset's deep voice crackles over the ancient loudspeaker during the morning announcements.

Next to me, Connor is making kissy-lips at Sheila across the desk square. I want to puke all over them; these two are too sugary sweet for human consumption. I picture what it would be like to dance with Connor—even though I don't dance—and imagine everyone clapping and cheering us on, and I'd be happy that Connor's moved on from that girl and found his true love, and I'd also be happy I didn't go to the dance with Little Miss Roadkill after all. I have the strongest urge to tell Dad, *"I'm going to the dance with Connor Flipping Garcia, who's nice and kind and also a boy, and not June, who is none of those things."* My hand is halfway to my pocket before I remember, oh right, none of that actually happened, Connor is straight, and I am not a girl; and going with June means Dad will let me apply to the Gladstone Art Academy; and neither she nor my parents know I'm gay. Such is life in the real world, where I am not an anime boy fighting a gigantic dragon. But I do the best I can anyway.

* * *

Swimming class is uneventful today—more laps, more strokes, more Coach Streit blowing her whistle. Odin sits atop the bleachers again, and it looks like he's still sketching away at his dragon.

As we file back into the locker room to rinse off and change, I see Ron out of the corner of my eye talking to someone by one of the benches. Careful not to make eye contact, I change back into my clothes, but I wind up overhearing Ron's conversation.

"So I said to the guy," Ron says, "'No, I don't want to go to the school musical with you. What are you, some kind of homo?'"

The other guy laughs. "What'd he say?"

"He was like, 'Nah, man, I ain't gay.' Then I was like, 'No, you just like watching dudes in costumes and makeup prance around onstage. Not gay at all!' That's the problem with gays—they keep showing up everywhere and shoving themselves in our faces. We can't catch a break."

My hands start shaking.

"It's not right," Ron continues. "Dudes shouldn't be with dudes. Gay guys shouldn't be allowed to use the same locker room as straight guys. I don't want some homo peeping at me. You know?"

"Nobody would look at you, Ron," I say, "because nobody likes to stare at bigots."

There's a horrible, horrible pause where it occurs to me that I didn't think that sentence. I said it out loud. From behind me Ron grabs my shirt and pulls me to face him. "What," he says, very slowly, "did you say to me?"

"Easy, Ron," his friend says.

But Ron is past the point of reason. "What did you call me, Galan?"

I swallow. My whole body is trembling. "A b-b-b-bigot."

"And what . . . the *hell* . . . is that?"

Oh my God. He doesn't know. He doesn't know I called him a homophobe, an insensitive jerk, an intolerant pain. The sheer irony of it, of Ron not understanding a word about not understanding, is so funny that it cracks the tension with a sledgehammer, and I laugh.

And then I'm on the floor.

And my face is on fire.

Searing, throbbing pain spreads across my face from a freight train crashing into my eye, and I try to cover my head but I can't see anything, and the omnipresent screaming and clattering all around me shatters my ears, and all of a sudden there are hands all over my body, trying to lift me up, yanking me from side to side, clanging my body against the nearby bench, and there are so many voices directly above me, and there is a shrill, piercing whistle that blasts what's left of my eardrums, and above it all Coach Streit barks, "*Get away from him!*"

By the time the whistle fades from my ears, I'm being lifted to my feet, so shaky I can barely stand on my own, and everything is white, but my hand is still against my eye, pressing down as if it can stem the lightning bolts of pain cascading from it in waves. There is so much noise around me; everyone is yelling, no one is still.

"Everyone finish changing and stand in a single file line outside the locker room," Coach Streit continues as I'm led toward the doors. "Except *you*," she thunders at an unseen person. "You and anyone who can tell me what happened. Mitchell, get Cole to the nurse's office, pronto."

I trip over anything and everything in my way while someone—Marcellus?—keeps me steady. As we leave, I hear a voice say, "I can tell you exactly what happened."

We exit the locker room—I think—and I stumble out into the hallway, but I'm kept steady. "Easy," Marcellus's voice says. "I got you." The way he says it is so comforting, so strong, I let him lead the way.

After a little while I can see again, but the throbbing agony in my left eye is still all-powerful. I'm shaky, and I might throw up breakfast. Only when we arrive at the nurse's office, right as the bell rings, do I open my mouth, which feels wedged with cotton. I try to ask what happened, only to experience an unpleasant gurgling sensation in place of words.

Nurse Hernandez rushes over and stretches me out on a bed. I overhear her and Marcellus talking, and Marcellus says the words, "He got punched pretty bad." Is that what happened? All I remember is laughing at something, and then I was on the floor, and—and—

The nurse gives me an ice pack for my eye and the next few minutes are a blur, and then I find myself next to Principal Dorset, ice pack clutched to my face like my eye will fall out if I remove it (which is what it feels like), and Coach Streit is there, and another guy it takes me a second to recognize as Odin, who's going on about what he saw (which is all news to me): Ron grabbing me by the shirt, me laughing at something, Ron decking me and trying to pick me back up again, Marcellus and Coach Streit intervening.

"Alan?" Principal Dorset asks very kindly. "Is this true?"

I guess it's true. I don't remember any of it. The principal seems to sense my ambivalence and takes it for a yes. And—

Oh man. Oh my God. Ron hit me. Ron punched me in the face. Because—because I'm—

Now I'm definitely going to throw up.

Principal Dorset mutters to Coach Streit that he'll need to call my parents—

Oh. Crap. "Nnnnnnnononono," I slur. "Don't call my parents. Please."

Principal Dorset looks at Coach Streit, and both adults look at me with what, in my blurry vision, vaguely resembles sympathy. In the chair next to me, Odin watches me carefully.

"Your parents need to be informed," Principal Dorset finally says. "When one of them arrives, we'll discuss what happened further. Okay?"

But it's not okay. If they find out why I got into this fight—if they know why Ron punched me—

As awful as I feel right now, I'm about to feel a whole lot worse.

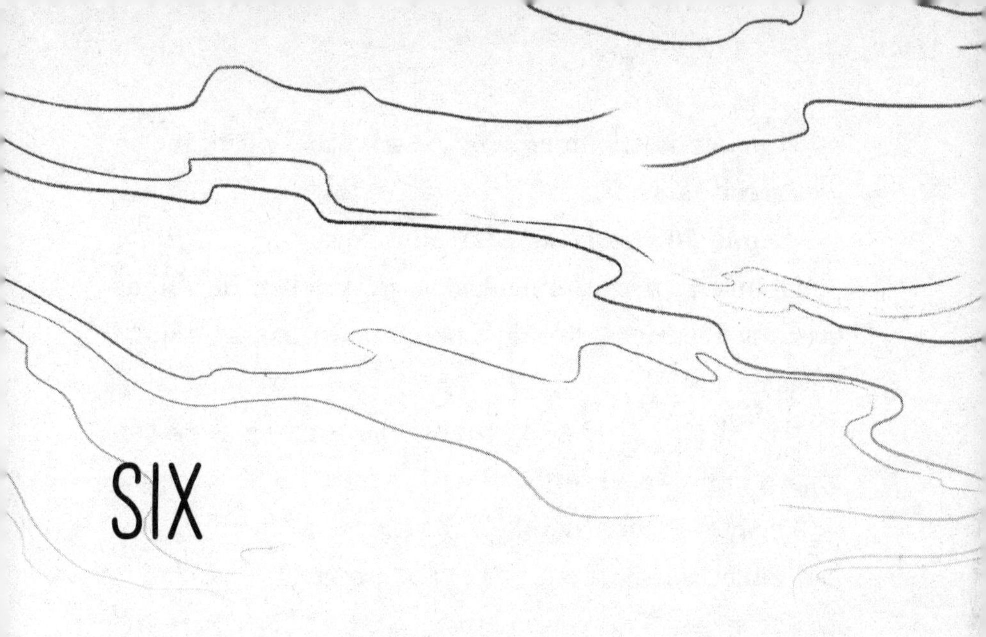

SIX

Principal Dorset and Coach Streit leave the nurse's office, but Marcellus and Odin stick around. "You two should get back to class," Nurse Hernandez says. "He'll be fine without you here."

I'm sprawled over a bed, still woozy and dizzy and nauseous, but I think I've gotten my body more fully under control. Marcellus is watching me, but Odin has gotten out his unlined paper and has now moved on to coloring his dragon with colored pencils. "I'd rather stay," Marcellus says. "Until his family gets here."

"What about you?" the nurse asks Odin.

Odin shrugs but doesn't look up.

"Fine," Nurse Hernandez says. "I'll write you both passes—"

The door to the nurse's office screeches open and in walks Nathan.

"Family has arrived," Marcellus says.

I crane my neck to get a look at my brother. He stands over my bed, arms folded, looking down at me. "'Sup?" he asks.

"Hi," I say. My voice sounds like a dying duck collapsed in my vocal cords.

The nurse looks like she's about to say something, but Nathan cuts her off with, "I'm his brother."

She sighs. "Pass for you too."

Nathan shakes his head. A flash of concern sparks in his eyes, and his lip curves downward into a grimace of anxiety, but when he speaks, he's all bluster. "You can't go a day without getting into trouble, can you?"

I cough. "I learned from the best."

He smirks. It's surreal to have him speaking to me again. I guess all it took was the destruction of my face for him to remember he's got a little brother. He reaches out for my ice pack. "Let me see."

"Hey!" I yelp, but moving hurts, and he's able to remove the pack.

Nathan flinches. Marcellus whistles. Even Odin stops sketching to look over, muttering, "Yeesh."

"That bad, huh?" I ask.

"Let's put it this way," Nathan says. "If you want to

get out of going to the Winter Dance, here's your excuse."

"Wow, mean," Odin mutters.

Nathan jerks his thumb in Odin's direction. "Who's this?"

"New kid," Marcellus says. "Told the coach what happened. Let him be."

I reapply the ice pack. "Thanks, Odin," I say.

"I hate bullies," Odin says. "No one deserves to be picked on."

"And thank you too," I say to Marcellus. "For getting me here."

Marcellus shrugs. "Just filling in until big bro showed up."

"Whatever," Nathan says, shoving his hands in his pockets. He drags his tennis shoe along the tiles. "I showed up. Take it or leave it."

I try to smile. I almost succeed, but it's the thought that counts. "I'll take it."

Against the wall, Marcellus says, "Me too." Marcellus Mitchell: surrogate big brother, waiting until the real one got the courage to do his job.

"Is Mom coming?" Nathan asks.

If I'd managed to smile before, it would've faded away immediately.

Nathan starts pacing. "What are you going to tell her?"

I swallow. Or at least I try to. "I don't know."

"They're going to find out eventually," he says. "You know that, right?"

I sigh. "I know. I guess I was hoping it'd be . . ." It'd be what exactly? Never?

Odin stops sketching for a few seconds. "So did that jerk say the truth? Are you gay?"

"None of your business, new kid," Nathan says, hovering dangerously close to Odin's drawing. "Worry about yourself."

"Did I look like I was talking to you?" Odin asks.

Nathan raises his eyebrows. "You ever experienced the inside of a toilet before?"

My eyes bulge out (which really hurts—ow). "Nathan!" I groan.

My brother sits down on the adjacent bed. "Sorry. Old habits."

Odin rolls his eyes. "Well?" he asks me.

"Yeah," I say. "I'm . . . gay."

For a few seconds Odin observes me. "Okay," he says. Then he goes back to sketching.

"All right," Nurse Hernandez says. "You've all been here long enough. Time to go back to cl—"

"Alan!"

Madison barges into the nurse's office. "What happened? Are you hurt? Everyone's talking about—" He sees all the people by my bed and freezes. Specifically, he sees Nathan by my bed and freezes. Nathan, the guy who made *Fatison* a schoolwide nickname.

"And who are you?" Nurse Hernandez asks with a sigh. "Cousin?"

Madison draws himself up to his full height and speaks in the deepest voice he can muster. "I am Madison Wilson Truman, Alan Cole's best friend. I'm here for moral support, guidance, and, if necessary, protection." He scowls at Nathan.

With a sigh, Nurse Hernandez writes yet another pass. "Alan, you're quite the popular guy."

Popular? Me? It sure doesn't feel that way as I lie in this bed after some jerk beat me up. The sheer terror that still plays at my gut, along with the blinding whiteness and echoing screams, are reminders of how popular I really feel. But maybe a sign of true popularity is whether people are willing to stick by you in sickness and in health (though I guess the "'til death do us part" bit is asking too much).

"What happened?" Madison whispers, approaching me. "People are saying Ron McCaughlin beat you up in swimming. Is that true?"

"You don't have to whisper," Nathan says, lying down on the other bed. "Everyone can hear you."

Madison puffs out his cheeks. "Honestly. There is such a thing as privacy, thank you."

I take the ice pack off my eye. Madison recoils, then catches himself. "It doesn't look that bad." He points at Odin. "What's he doing here?"

"*Trying* to draw," Odin grumbles.

Madison scrunches his face up in disgust.

"I don't like the little twerp either," Nathan laughs. "But hey, can't control the company your brother keeps. Am I right?"

A squeaking noise comes out of Madison's mouth, like a teakettle about to blow. "I've done more for Alan over the past month than you've done your whole life."

I prop my head up. "Madison," I whisper. "Don't."

Whatever I expect Nathan to do next, he doesn't do it. Instead of quipping with a comeback or threatening Madison or acting like an insufferable, cocky know-it-all, he lies on the bed in silence. He closes his eyes.

Madison looks at me, then at Nathan. Marcellus looks up from his phone.

Eventually Nathan says, faintly, "I'm here now. I . . . promise."

Nathan always keeps his promises. Even during CvC games and complete torture, if he promised he was going to do something, he did it. I know he doesn't make promises lightly. The old Cole family motto, from before Nathan and I were born, bubbles up from my brain: *Today, do your best.*

A silence falls over the nurse's office, broken periodically by Odin's colored pencils. Then—

"Alan!"

Nurse Hernandez throws her hands into the air. "That's it. I'm not writing you a pass. You can go back to class."

"Oh, that's okay," Zack says. "I've got a bathroom pass. Mr. Dunlap is probably going to think I'm taking the world's longest pee though. Wow, hi, everyone!"

By now the nurse's office is packed tight. Madison squeezes in next to Odin, and Zack hustles in next to Marcellus. "I told you you'd make friends with Odin," Zack says, smiling.

Zack and Madison and I all wind up talking about what happened, and both of them are horrified, and it's like the three of us didn't fight at all. Eventually Madison asks, "What are you going to tell your parents?"

I've made up my mind about this. "I'll tell them I got into an argument. I don't have to say what it was about."

"That won't work," Nathan chimes in, relaxing on the other bed like he owns the thing. "Dad's going to want to know what was worth getting a black eye over."

"Then I'll make something up," I say. "Ron threatened to steal my lunch money. Ron didn't like a TV show I watch. Ron thought my hair was ugly."

"Your hair *is* ugly," Nathan says. "Maybe it'd help if

I roughed this kid up a little. We could say you did it. Then Dad would at least think you fought back."

"Yes, that's a great idea," Madison says with an eye roll. "Let's send three of his fingers to his parents."

Nathan grins. "Now you're getting in the spirit."

"Do you really think your parents will react that bad if you tell them?" Zack asks.

My eye throbs again. "Call me a weirdo, but I don't want to broadcast this right now." And a sudden, terrifying realization overwhelms me: I don't want *anyone* to know. Not just Mom and Dad—the whole world. I came out to practically the entire school at once, so there were never any gradual steps, at least at Evergreen. But now I . . . I want to hide it. I want to hide under the covers and stay there for weeks. I want to not get punched anymore by bigots who think gay people have nothing better to do than plot against straight people. I would *love* to be straight! I would love to walk down the street holding hands with a girl and not have to worry about getting taunted or punched! Why wouldn't I?

I would love to go to a dance with a girl and not have to worry about anything.

I lie back on the pillow and close my eyes.

A silence hangs in the air before Odin says, "I told the principal and the gym teacher you got into an argument about who had the better backstroke. Not about what actually happened."

"They bought that?" I croak.

"They wanted the real reason," Odin says, "but I wouldn't tell them."

I sit up.

Odin's scratching pencils fill the room.

"Thanks," I say.

We lock eyes. "You're welcome," he says.

Then Mom is standing at the foot of my bed, and it's time to go home.

To what, I have no idea.

SEVEN

So, first things first: I look terrible.

After Mom and I talk with Principal Dorset and Coach Streit, we walk to the car, and I check myself out in the mirror, and yep—that's a black eye. Well, it's more puffy and red than black, but I have a feeling it'll darken soon enough. It throbs so bad I expect my actual skin to pulsate. I picture Mom giving me a gigantic raw steak to cover it, and that's when she starts crying. Sitting in the driver's seat, with the car turned off, crying.

And I do not know what to do. In all the years Mom's been, well, Mom, I've never seen her cry. She spiraled into the deepest, dankest dungeons of depression, and she never cried, maybe because she was beyond crying—she would have had to feel emotion to cry. But now she's a functioning human being again, and she has emotions and oh my God I did this, I totally did this, I made my own mother cry. I open my mouth, but nothing comes out. If this is how Mom reacts, I can't wait to see what Dad thinks.

"Does it hurt?" Mom whispers.

"Huh?"

She reaches over and cups my face. Her touch doesn't soothe me; her hands feel like warped plastic draped over my chin. She shakes her head and lets out a mighty sob. "I can't believe they did this to you."

She didn't seem to have a problem when it was Nathan doing the beating, but that might have been because Nathan never left marks. I know that's a mean thing to think, but hey, it's true.

"I thought," she says, her crying coming faster and harder now, "I thought we could—we could have left this b-behind. I thought you c-c-could have a l-l-life without fighting n-now."

"There are always jerks," I say. "Family or not."

Mom removes her hands from my chin. She blows her nose and takes a few deep breaths. I don't say anything. Anything I say will make it worse. Does she know the real reason behind the fight? Can she tell? "Oh, Alan," she sighs. "What am I going to do with you?"

Take me home! Take me home so I can crawl into bed and never leave.

She finally starts up the car and drives away from Evergreen. The air is thick and not because she's been crying.

Before I know it, we're home. As we leave the car, I stand in front of the doorway. "Don't tell Dad. Please."

"He's going to know when he sees you."

"Make up something. He doesn't need to know I got in a fight." Or why.

"Alan, he needs to know what's going on," she says, walking past me and opening the door. "He's your father."

I don't walk inside right away. "You haven't known what's going on with me for twelve years. Why start now?"

She runs her fingers over the cross around her neck. "Alan—"

A deep scream scrapes and claws its way out of my gut. *"I didn't do anything wrong!"* I run past Mom and thud my way upstairs, slam my door shut, huddle under my sheets, and let the weight of the day thunder over my shoulders. When someone punches you in the face, it isn't only your face that feels the pain. Your heart feels it too. Your soul. Your mind.

She doesn't know. But if she did, would she still love me the same amount? I can't bring myself to ask. I can't bring myself to confront the truth. I can't bring myself to hear the word *No*.

* * *

In the hours between leaving school and dinner, when Dad gets home, I go through phases. Sometimes my entire body seizes up like there's a set of scalding iron tongs compressed around my heart. Sometimes I'm faced with a Zen-like euphoria, and noble conclusions fill my mind about how I'm overreacting, everything will be fine, Dad won't disown me. Mostly I sit in bed with my bestie the ice pack, and imagine myself as a potato, squatting like a lump until someone peels away my skin.

Zack and Madison keep texting me to see if I'm okay. At one point I text both of them:

not up for talking. will see you both tomorrow. if I'm still alive.

Then, because I don't want to give them the wrong idea that this potato wants to mash himself, I text back:

that was a joke. head's still woozy. sorry.

At some point school must get out, because Nathan knocks at my door. "Hey, Black Eye Bill, you awake in there?" he calls. "I brought you something."

I let out a pathetic groan.

Nathan opens the door anyway. "Hey!" I yelp.

"Tough love," he says. "Wow, your face looks even worse than it did at school. That's impressive."

I throw a pillow at him.

He tries to play hacky sack with it, but it winds up falling to the floor quickly. "Anyway," he says, "I brought you all the homework you missed! Aren't I a good brother?"

A lot of my classes do online homework, so this is mostly stuff from Mrs. Ront, my English teacher, who refuses to modernize. As I look over the papers, Nathan asks, "How'd it go?"

"She cried."

"Yikes. Mom never cries."

"Well, I made her cry. With my gayness."

Nathan leans toward me. "She was probably upset that you got your face punched in. I would be too. I mean, have you looked in the mirror lately? Besides, she doesn't even know."

"Not yet."

"That twerp friend of yours did something good by lying. She doesn't know. It's going to be okay."

I groan again. "Dad is going to kill me."

"Why would Dad care? He doesn't know. Neither of them knows! You're all panicky from being turned into tenderized meat. Just relax."

My eye throbs, even through the ice pack. *Relax*, he says. "Maybe . . . maybe I should tell them."

"Now? With one of your eyes dangling out of its socket?"

"Will you stop with the face jokes?"

"I mean, like I said, they're going to find out eventually. If you tell them now, maybe you'll earn sympathy points from looking like a Halloween mask."

I bury my face under the covers. "I want to be by myself. Thanks for the homework."

"Fine, but sulking in your room isn't going to change anything. If you want to sulk, I won't stop you, but the world doesn't have time for sulkers. And my brother doesn't sulk. He gets things done."

I sit up. Did he say—did Nathan pay me a compliment?

Then the front door slams shut.

All Nathan's bravado drains from his face, and his true concern is unmasked for the first time.

Of course Dad comes home early today. Because my timing is *exquisite.*

Nathan looks back at me once, then leaves my room.

And I know what I must do. Nathan's right: I don't sulk. The Alan I know marches forward with confidence. I slowly sit up and make my way downstairs, where I can hear Dad and Mom talking in the kitchen. In . . . out . . . in . . . out . . .

"Alan!" Dad calls, unaware that I'm standing in the doorway.

"Hi," I say weakly. I didn't bring my ice pack, and my head is throbbing.

Dad turns white. He rushes over and puts his hands on my shoulders, making me wince. He slowly wraps me up in a hug and holds me for a little while.

Eventually he breaks the hug and looks me over. "You've done it this time," he says. "It's a good thing you've already got a date for your dance."

I don't say anything. Taking June to this stupid dance is the last thing on my mind right now. Even the art academy feels like a lifetime ago.

Dad whistles. "What in the world did you do to get a shiner like that?"

My heart stops. I look at Mom, clutching her hands to her heart. But now it falls on me. In . . . out . . . "I, uh, well, I—"

Dad unpacks his briefcase, but it's clear he's still listening.

"This guy, uh, he and, uh, me, we got into an argument—"

"Bah!" Dad waves his hand. "Typical hotheaded kids. After I learned to fight, I got into plenty of scrapes when I was your age over the dumbest things—"

Tell him. Tell him. Tell him tell him tell him tell him tell him—

"—one time we fought over who could hold our breath the longest. My friend wouldn't believe I could hold it for four minutes, so he shoved me onto the ground, and next thing I know, I'm bleeding from the lip in three places! Good times. What did you fight about?"

I try to swallow but my mouth is too dry. I look at Dad, then Mom. Slime threatens to tumble out of my belly and up through my throat. Finally, I croak out, "We got into an argument over—over who had the better backstroke." Immediately my eyes drop to the floor. I try to ignore the wetness pooling behind them.

Dad laughs gruffly. "That's it? Kids are the dumbest. Right, Cindy?"

Mom doesn't say anything.

"I hope you gave him one back," Dad says. "Someone punches me in the face, you better believe they're going to get a punch in return."

"He shouldn't be fighting at all," Mom says.

"Unless he's provoked. Which he was. If you want to impress girls like June Harrison, you need to be willing to throw a punch when you need to."

The wetness is leaking out of the corners of my eyes. It stings. "I'll be in my room," I whisper, and I fly up the stairs before either of my parents can say another word. I fly into my room and fly into my bed and try to fly away from the truth.

Not today. Not when I'd rather bury my head in sand than look up at the sun. I'll tell them eventually.

Hopefully.

* * *

Dinner is silent, as usual, except for the ticking and tocking of Dad's old wooden clock, a family heirloom that hangs in the kitchen. We focus on eating our bucket of fried chicken like it's the most important thing in the universe. My plate only has two drumsticks, barely touched.

"Nathan, how was your day today?" Mom asks.

Nathan burps. "It was okay. We're finally dissecting real frogs in science, so that's cool."

"Did you buy a ticket for your dance yet?" Dad asks.

Nathan looks down at his plate. "I'm not going. Dances are stupid."

"I want both my kids going to this dance," Dad says. "It's important to put out a good impression. That's why Alan isn't going to that silly art academy anymore."

I drop my fork. "Wh-What? Why?"

"I'd rather spend the money on fighting lessons," Dad says. "So you can defend yourself like a real man."

Heat claws out of my body from every pore. "I don't want to fight," I spit out. I can't believe I'm hearing this. I can't apply to Gladstone because I got beat up?

"You will," Dad says. "Girls love fighters."

"Jimmy, he's only twelve," Mom says. "He's been through a lot today. Can we talk about this more tomorrow?"

"We're talking about it now, aren't we?" Dad asks.

Mom's eyes drop to the table.

"Why can't I still go to Gladstone?" I ask. "You're punishing me for getting punched?"

"It's a better investment," Dad says. "Art isn't a good way to spend your time. We've been over this before."

"Dad, come on," Nathan mutters quietly. "That's not fair."

Dad glares at my brother. "I don't care what's fair. I care about what's good. My parents"—he takes a great gulp of water—"never wanted me to fight. They said fighting was bad. If you fight, you're nothing more than an animal. When I came home with scrapes and cuts from bullies, they never taught me to stand up for myself. I had to learn to cut down anyone who stood in my way. I'm doing you a favor by making you stand up for yourself. Next time this kid picks a fight with you, it would be good of you to fight back."

I can barely think straight. Words are floating near my mouth in disjointed half sentences. "I'm not—I'm not a fighter. I'm an artist."

"You're not a fighter or an artist right now," Dad rumbles. "Right now you're a loser. And you're going to win. Whether you like it or not."

I stand up so quickly my knees bang the table. Dizzy, nauseous, left eye throbbing, I stomp away from the table and march into my room and slam the door shut.

Loser.

My own father just called me a loser.

My own father wants to deny me my reason for existing because some jerk at school decided to use my face as target practice for his fists.

I can't even begin to imagine what he would say if he knew I was gay.

I don't know what time it is when my bedroom door opens a crack. I must have fallen asleep. I pretend I still am.

"Hey," Nathan whispers.

I don't say anything.

"Hang in there," he says. He shuts the door.

Sure. Hang in there. I'll hang in there tomorrow. When morning comes, and it's time to become a functioning human being again, I'll come back to life and do my best to meet the eyes of the sun. For now, though, the rest of the world can carry on without Alan Cole for a few hours. And for now, Alan Cole is perfectly happy to carry on without the rest of the world.

EIGHT

For a school as huge as Evergreen, word gets around fast when something big happens. From the moment I board bus 19 on Tuesday, people are whispering and pointing and staring. I guess it's hard to miss the guy with the wrecked face, but even if I looked like a supermodel, people would still know.

There goes the kid that got beat up for being gay.

I was already sort of used to the stares after I came out, but those had mostly gone away once people got accustomed to sharing the halls with a gay kid. But now they're back in full force. Everyone turns their head to get a glimpse of me. And usually they turn away as soon as they see the black eye—which is now a fully fledged blue and purple monstrosity—like they've never watched a boxing match before. (Except most boxing matches don't end in one punch.) One thing I learn from the whispers: Ron got suspended. So I won't have to worry about him, at least for a little while. Small comfort.

I walk by the community bulletin board and get lost in all the clubs, clubs for the kids who are comfortable with who they are. After yesterday, I don't want to even get out of bed, let alone go to a club.

"Hey, watch it!"

I bump into someone: Odin. "Uh, sorry," I stammer.

He doesn't look at me. He's busy admiring something on the board: the Gladstone flyer. "I'm going to that," he says.

"You got accepted?" I ask. Oh no, did their deadline pass already, and I somehow missed it? That would be the icing on the poison cake.

"They won't send out acceptances for a few weeks. But I'm going. I know it."

Whew. "I'd like to go too," I say in the biggest understatement of the century. "Maybe we'll both get in." If Dad even lets me apply anymore. But Odin doesn't have to know that.

"We can't both get in. They take one student per school. That's it."

Huh? That's news to me. Sure enough, in tiny print at the bottom, it says:

The Gladstone Art Academy, in its commitment to cultural and geographic diversity, regretfully can only accept one student per school.

Once every three years, and they only take one student per school?

"Looks like you're not going," Odin says. "'Cause I am."

"You know," I say, feeling a hot wave of anger pulse through me, "you don't have to be such a jerk all the time."

Odin frowns. "I'm not a jerk."

"That's news to me." I roll my eyes (which I immediately regret—ouch) and walk away. On the way to homeroom I pass by Talia's "Where Do We Come From?" display, which is up to five "stories." Three of them are art pieces, one is a photograph, and one is a poem. I imagine my cretpoj hanging there—not the first time I've imagined this—and picture all the admirers who'd stare at me because of my amazing artistic skills, not because I'm a helpless gay kid who got beaten up by a homophobe. If I don't go to the art academy, though, is there even a point? The academy is for serious artists. I can't even share one painting with the world. Maybe Dad's got a point. Maybe I'm more of a loser than an artist.

As I glance over the art, I notice a familiar-looking picture: a warrior and a dragon, in anime style. Odin's picture he spent yesterday finishing. The anime boy has his short, curly hair. So does the dragon.

"Pretty great, huh?" Odin says from behind me.

I nod, trying to curb my rage from earlier. But in the place of rage manifests a new emotion, one I can't immediately place. Odin is so comfortable with his art that he can walk around with designs all over his jacket and flaunt his pictures in the halls. He'll probably brag to anyone within earshot he's going to the art academy. And his stuff is good. Like, really good.

Is this . . . am I . . . jealous of him?

As if I didn't need any more reasons to hate myself.

"Alan!" someone calls, and Connor is walking up to me. An expression I've never seen on him before fills his face. "Oh man, look at you," he mutters. "I can't believe that stupid little—"

Remember how I said all the words I could use to describe Ron were unprintable? Connor just taught me a new one.

I don't reply. Instead I bask in Connor's attentions, something I haven't been getting any of for weeks. Part of me wonders if I have to get beaten up to get my crush to notice me (and an incredibly annoying part of me wonders if it's worth it, but that part gets silenced pretty quickly).

"I'm sorry, man," Connor says. "I said I'd protect you from Ron, and I blew it. You must hate me."

I want to say I could never hate you, Connor Garcia, you and your big smile, but instead I say, "It's okay. It's not your responsibility."

Odin, of course, has to ruin the moment. "You're the bully defender? Where the heck were you yesterday then?"

Connor looks at Odin like he's just noticed him. "I don't have swimming with Alan and Ron. But I should've stepped in sooner. I'm really sorry—"

"I bet you are," Odin grumbles.

That hot wave of anger reappears. This time I can't keep it down. "Shut up, Odin."

"Why are you defending him?" Odin asks. "He didn't protect you. I mean, you clearly can't protect yourself."

"Don't you think *I know that*?" I scream. A silence falls over the hall. I stomp past Connor and Odin into homeroom, thudding into my desk.

Zack has arrived early today. He's talking to Jenny Cowper about the dance—I overhear him say, "He's a great guy, you two would have a great time"—and Jenny laughs and ignores him. Zack is either clueless about who would be a good fit for Madison (Jenny hates Madison's guts), or he's so desperate to find Madison any date, he's willing to take anyone into consideration. He and Madison both come over to my desk. "How do you feel?" Zack asks.

"Like a million bucks."

"Did your parents . . . ?" Madison asks.

Odin takes the desk next to me and flips open a book. "I didn't tell them," I say, ignoring his presence. "But my dad wants me to take fighting lessons instead of going to the art academy."

Madison's face falls. "That's completely ridiculous. He's being a Neanderthal. And they even had time for art in the Stone Age!"

"Does this mean you still have to take that girl to the dance?" Zack asks.

Dad said as much to me in the morning. "Don't think you're getting out of taking June Harrison," he grumbled as I brushed my teeth. "Buy your ticket today." Then he was out the door, ready to acquire more fatherly pearls of wisdom for future encounters with his children.

"Yeah," I groan. "My dad is obsessed with me dating girls."

"Well," Madison says hesitantly, "maybe it's good that you're trying them out then—"

I glare at Madison, and he stops talking.

"I know a good way to get our minds off bad stuff," Zack says. "Let's come up with girls me and Madison can ask to the dance."

"I can't believe you're still doing this," Madison sighs. "You asked Jenny Cowper. She despises me."

"She needs to get to know you."

"She needs a new middle school, far away from here."

Zack ignores Madison. "Alan, since you're going to the dance with a girl, do you know anyone we can ask?"

He doesn't mean anything by it. I know he doesn't. That only makes it worse. "I wouldn't, no."

The sheer iciness of my words silences both of my friends. Eventually Zack says, "Well, think it over, okay?" and walks back to his desk.

Right when I reach for my bestie the ice pack, my phone vibrates. Who could be texting me during school? I look around the room and hide my phone under my desk. The message reads:

Hello, Alan. <3

I know better than to respond to mysterious text messages from numbers I don't recognize. A few seconds later, another message pops up:

Are you excited to go to the dance with me?

Crap. Crap crap craaaaap. I text back:

hi june. don't you have school now? because I do.

School is an illusion. I've got a free period next. I'll call you in half an hour and we can talk about plans. Okie-dokie?

What? But I don't have a free period next. Before I can text her this important bit of information, Miss Richter says, "Phones away, please," and that's that. Great.

During the morning announcements, Principal Dorset says, "I would like to take this moment to remind everyone here that bullying or intolerance of any kind, for any reason, is strictly prohibited. Evergreen Middle School is a place of inclusion and acceptance, not bigotry. If anyone feels bullied or observes bullying in action, please notify a teacher immediately. No one deserves—"

Everyone keeps looking at me. They know who this is about. I tune the speech out.

When the bell rings, Miss Richter calls me over to her desk. I walk slowly, hoping that maybe she'll change her mind once I'm halfway there. She doesn't. "How are you feeling?" she asks.

I shrug.

"I want you to know you can always come to me," she says. "This is a safe space. Okay?"

"Okay."

She examines me carefully. "You're not blaming yourself, are you?"

Why is she always so good at this? "Uh, no."

"Alan, you've done nothing wrong. I want you to repeat after me: I've done nothing wrong."

I don't say anything.

"Repeat after me: I've done nothing wrong."

I look down. "I've . . . I've . . ." I try to swallow. "I've got to get to first period."

I flee out the door before Miss Richter can call out to me.

Maybe I haven't done anything wrong. Maybe I could have done everything differently. But there's one thing I do know: things are different now. Things have always been unknown and scary to some extent, but now they're beyond that. Now they're *critical.* This is a critical situation in dangerous waters. And I've got to figure out how to say afloat.

Halfway through swimming class I ask to be excused to the locker room. Of course, I could ignore the call. But if I know June, it's best to rip off the Band-Aid as quickly as possible. I make it to my locker just in time to hear the vibrations, and I try not to get too much water on my phone as I answer. "Yeah?"

"Wow, I'm impressed," June's voice comes over the other end. "You found a private spot."

"I can't talk for long," I say, trying to keep my voice down to stem the echoes all around me. "What do you want?"

"Oh, you know, just to chitchat, talk about the

weather and local sports teams. Baseball certainly is a sport, isn't it?"

"It is taking every ounce of willpower I have to not hang up on you."

"Okay, sheesh. Guess you're the type to hold a grudge."

"Do you even know what my dad did to me after that company dinner? Do you even care?"

"Of course I care. I am a very caring, compassionate person." She giggles. "I taught you a lesson about how everyone is bad, didn't I?"

I open my mouth, but no sound comes out. With everything that's happened in the past twenty-four hours, June's philosophy of "people are inherently bad" seems more and more accurate. But I'd never admit that to her.

"Did your dad tell you the news?" she asks. "That we're going to the Winter Dance together?"

I sigh. "Yeah."

"You don't sound thrilled. I want to hear it from you. We are going to the dance together, yes?"

I've made my decision.

Here's what I'm thinking: taking June somehow still might get me Dad's approval to go to Gladstone Art Academy, and that's almost worth the price of admittance, even though I don't like girls, and even though I don't like *her* as a human being. But this might help Dad with his promotion, and if Dad is happy, there's a stronger chance I won't be unhappy, and there's also a strong chance he'll be able to afford sending me to Gladstone in the first place. Also, this might be the only opportunity I'd have to go to the academy in three years, plus I could really use something to look forward to, especially something that could prove I'm still an artist. And even more than all of this, there's the fact that I'd be going with a *girl*, and it would be nice to not be stared at or taunted or threatened by half the people in attendance. So, keeping all that in mind . . .

"I'll go with you."

"Sounds good to me. Maybe we can turn the evening into something special."

"Yeah, sure. Got to go. Bye, June."

"So long, partner. See you real soon . . ."

I get chills up my spine, and they're not because I'm still dripping wet.

As I stand up from the bench, I look up—and Odin's there. "Who was that?" he asks.

"None of your business," I grumble.

"Did you just agree to go to the dance with a girl?"

"I said none of your business, okay? Why don't you take your chlorine allergy and go back to the bleachers?"

Odin watches me, face blank. He leaves the locker room, with me close behind, ready for another few minutes of laps, strokes, and Coach Streit blowing her whistle. The wriggling worm of doubt nestles inside my brain, writhing around in my cerebellum, making me twitch in the water.

The Winter Dance table is set up prominently in the cafeteria, staffed by members of the Winter Dance committee, which I wasn't aware was a thing until today. There are committees for everything in this school. It wouldn't surprise me if there was a committee dedicated to maintaining the soap dispensers in the bathrooms or uncreasing the corners of pages in textbooks.

At the Unstable Table, Zack is going on about some fantastical story about a chameleon and a hunter who go on adventures together. I'm not listening, and I don't think Madison is either. Eventually I'm jostled out of my zombie-like trance, staring at the ticket table, by a strong "Alan Cole."

"Hi," I say glumly.

"I need your assistance," Talia says.

"Ooh, Talia!" Zack perks up like a puppy about to go for a walk. "What would you say if I told you—"

"Be quiet," Talia says, holding up a finger toward Zack's mouth. Then, to me, "I'm trying to put together an anti-bullying task force. I really want to speak out about this sort of thing."

"Okay," I say.

"You could be the face of bullying at Evergreen. Literally. It would do wonders for my publicity."

I take a deep breath. Then another. Then a third. "Talia."

Talia nods. "Yes, I think this is a great idea too."

"I don't want anything to do with this."

"What?" Talia stares at me like I told her that if you read the periodic table backwards you'll unlock "bonus elements" (which is what Zack told me the other day). "I don't understand. Why would you not want to do this?"

I sigh. "If you got punched in the face and everyone kept—kept staring at you all day, wouldn't you just want to do your own thing? To not be bothered?"

Talia pushes up her glasses. "I'll never understand you, Alan Cole."

"Hey, Talia!" Zack senses his opening. "How'd you like to go to the Winter Dance with Madison?"

Madison and Talia look at each other for a few seconds. Then they both crack up.

"Very funny," Madison says.

"That's a good one," Talia says.

"I'm serious," Zack says.

Talia stops laughing. "Go with Madison? Why?"

"Well, he needs a date, and you need a date, so I thought—"

Talia leans into the Unstable Table, knocking the

piece of cardboard out from its usual spot under the uneven leg; the table buckles and my tray almost flies into my lap. "Zack Kimble," Talia says, "what makes you think I need a date?"

Zack opens and closes his mouth a few times. "I, uh, thought you'd—"

"Nice try," Talia says, walking away.

Zack shakes his head. "This isn't going so good. We need to branch out to the Sprouts. Maybe even the Shrubs. Don't worry, Madison."

"I'm not worried," Madison says glumly. "You're the only one who's worried."

"That's because it's important!" Zack nods decisively. "I'll find you a date, or my name's not Emperor Snozbreath of Alpha Robotauri." He pauses. "By the way, I forgot to mention I'm changing my name to Emperor Snozbreath—"

"Excuse me?"

A girl stands at the head of the table, where Talia had been only moments ago. Zack freezes like a deer in cryogenic storage.

"Hello, Meredith," Madison says, sounding shocked that such a big gear in the seventh-grade political machine has chosen to speak to us lowly cogs. "How can we help you?"

Meredith Wood smiles. I can tell what Zack sees in

her. She's not exactly my type, but even I can't help but get sucked in a little. "Hi, guys," she says.

I nod. She's pretty and friendly, sure, but I'm not feeling too social right now. I look past Meredith at the dance table, a knot bunched in my stomach.

Meredith fidgets. "I wanted to ask you—"

"Yes!" Zack bolts out of his seat, snapped from his full-body lockdown, and actually—I am not making this up—kneels on one knee in front of Meredith. "I would—I would love to go to the—the dance with you, Meredith! I pledge my heart to you." He spreads his arms and grins a grin that's so cheesy it's practically dripping mozzarella.

But Meredith doesn't return the gesture. "Um," she says, uncomfortable now that all the nearby tables are watching her. "I was, um, actually here for—"

"We'll get a limo," Zack continues, "and a corsage, and a bouquet of the finest flowers. It'll be the best night of your life! I promise—"

"—for Madison."

Me and Madison can't take our eyes off the spectacle that is Zack. "Sorry?" Madison asks, looking at Meredith. "What did you say?"

"Do you . . ." Meredith hesitates. "Want to go to the dance with me?"

Madison looks behind him, then back at Meredith.

He points at himself and mouths, "Me?"

She nods.

Zack topples onto the floor.

As a teacher runs over to make sure Zack's okay, Meredith says, "So do you want to?"

"Er, I, er," Madison stammers. He cranes his neck over the table to watch Zack slowly get to his feet. Then he looks at me. I hide my eyes behind my hair. Finally, Madison gulps and says, "I—s-s-sure, that would, er, be great."

Meredith smiles. "Great. Don't forget to buy your ticket. See you around."

I've never seen Madison blush as much as he is right now. He breathes heavily and dabs at his forehead. He leans over and whispers to me, "Did—did that just happen?"

I nod. "Congrats."

Zack finally regains his seat. "Well, she walked away before I could talk about the holographic watch I'm going to be wearing. I almost thought she asked Madison to the dance!"

"She did," I say.

Zack gulps. "She what?"

"I'm sorry, Zack," Madison says. "I didn't know what to say! It all happened so fast. Besides, it must have been a mistake. Popular girls like her aren't interested in chubby guys like me. She clearly had me confused with a different Madison. There's no way Meredith Wood wants to go to the dance with *Fatison.*"

"Yeah, that's right," Zack says, more to himself than anyone else. "We should work on getting you a real date."

"Zack!" I say. "She asked him, not you. Get over it." Before either of them can say anything else, I glance at the dance table. The line's almost empty. No time like the present.

"Where are you going?" Madison asks as I stand up.

To face my destiny. To claim my fate. "To buy a ticket."

The seventh grader (or Sapling, if you hate yourself) at the table asks, "How many tickets?"

June can buy her own ticket—I'm sure Broadleaf has its own Winter Dance committee, staffed by parallel universe versions of Evergreen students. My eye starts to throb. I picture myself dressed in uncomfortable clothes, pretending to be interested in a girl who got my sketchbook thrown in a fireplace. I picture the dance crowd not staring at me or laughing at me or calling me names. I picture myself going to Gladstone Art Academy, championed as the next great artistic prodigy, holding up my canvas to the sun, free from all those pesky nuggets of self-doubt, preparing to change the world. I picture my cretpoj hanging on the WDWCF? wall, taped over Odin's stupid dragon drawing. I picture

Mom happy and not crying, I picture Dad getting his promotion and us moving into a mansion (hey, dream big). I picture Zack, crestfallen and alone, and Madison, running on a treadmill instead of dancing while Meredith watches. I picture myself, caught in the middle again, caught between the identity I've chosen and the identity that's chosen me.

"Uh, how many tickets?" the girl at the table asks again.

I take a deep breath. "One."

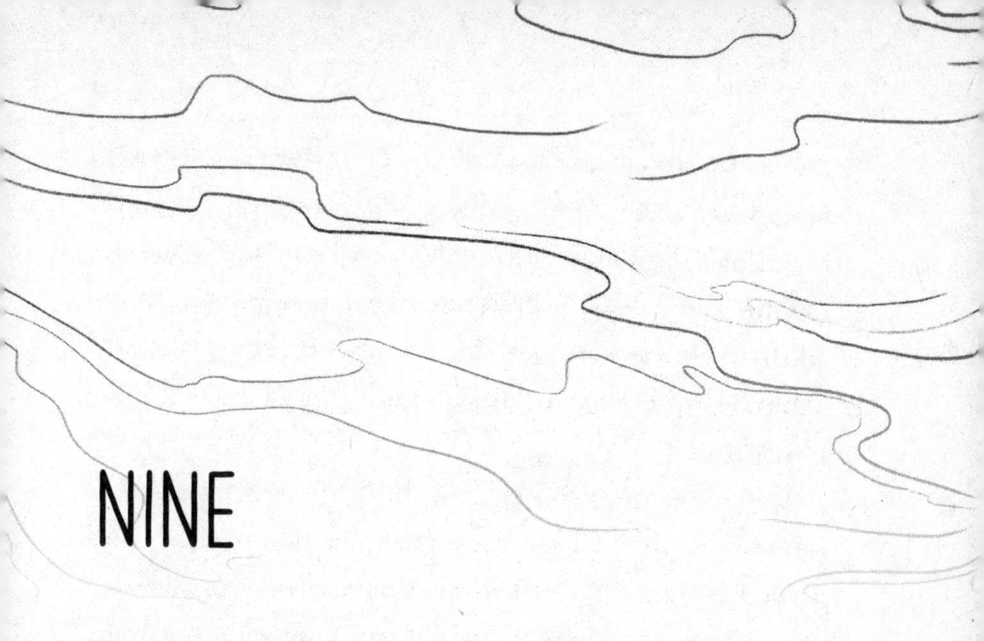

NINE

One week passes.

The thing about being the subject of rumors is eventually newer, more interesting rumors surge up and take your place, and you can return to being in the background. A high-profile humiliation, an athletic scandal, whatever you can think of, something always comes along to fill the gossip void. So I'm grateful for all the popular ninth graders who have very public, very messy breakups, and the feud between the marching band and the drama club, and even the installation of a new vending machine outside Miss Richter's room. Everyone's talking about them—which means everyone *isn't* talking about me.

It helps that ol' blue-and-purple is healing nicely. The swelling and discoloration have gone down. I've shelved my bestie the ice pack, until the day when his services are needed again, which hopefully won't be for quite some time. So I'm not as much of, as Talia so eloquently put it, "the face of bullying at Evergreen." Thankfully. Even though sometimes the eye still throbs, still pulsates, still acts as a painful reminder of how things really are.

Today, before school on this chilly Monday morning, I hand Mom our little secret: my application to the Gladstone Art Academy. Last week, Mom pulled me aside and said if I were to—hypothetically speaking—put together an application and—hypothetically speaking—leave it for her to mail today, then she could—hypothetically speaking—see that it finds its way into the mailbox. She said we'd worry about what happens if I get in (actually she said *when* I get in) once we reach that point. Hypothetically speaking, of course.

Inside my application is a faculty recommendation (which Mrs. Colton, my art teacher, was happy to provide) and a scanned copy of my cretpoj. It took me forever to actually place the self-portrait inside the darn envelope, but once I did, it felt final, like there was no going back. But I'm ready for this. I'm ready to learn and grow and change and get over my lousy blockage and for all the fun parts of going to a prestigious art academy.

And if I don't get in? Then . . . I try not to think about

what that says about my status as an artist, or how seriously I take art, or what I'm capable of doing as a human being. I try not to think about that, but I'm not successful.

At school Madison comes up to my locker and moans, "I was at Helen's Crest for seven hours yesterday. Seven hours! This is child abuse. I should call social services."

"You look like you're losing some weight though," I say.

Madison laughs bitterly. "Looks can be deceiving. I've lost two pounds in a month. That's nowhere near fifteen. My parents aren't happy. One more week of this, and the personal trainer makes an appearance."

"You should only put one foot on the scale," I say. "To confuse them."

Madison laughs again, but this time it's more genuine. "I think they're smarter than that."

"Next time shoot for dumber parents." I smile. It's one of the first real smiles I've made in a week. If this morning is any indication, things might be heading back to norma—

"Don't look now, Galan," someone says, giving me a light shove as they walk by. "Your best friend's back."

I turn red at the mention of my nickname, but I don't know what that guy's talking about. My best friends are Madison and Zack, and they never—

Oh crap.

At the other end of the hall, glaring fire through his eye sockets, is Ron.

Best friend.

He stares at me for what feels like hours. My muscles all lock up. Finally, he walks off.

I try to catch my breath. No such luck.

"What's he doing back here?" Madison gasps. "I thought he was suspended."

"Must've only been for a week," I say. Still trying to catch my breath. I knew a week was the standard suspension length, but I guess I was hoping for, say, two or three weeks. Or two or three years.

"Hey, did you guys see Ron's back?" Zack asks as we walk into homeroom. He looks at me. "Oh. Guess you did."

"Everyone's talking about it," Sheila Carter says. "You might want to hide, Alan. Ron looks pretty mad."

"Ron's not getting anywhere near Alan," Connor says, clapping me on the back. "He tries anything, and I'll kick the crap out of him."

"You tell him, honey," Sheila says. She blows Connor a kiss.

Zack wedges in between me and Connor. "You can handle him," Zack whispers to me. "He's no Nathan."

The words sink in a few minutes later, during the morning announcements: *He's no Nathan.*

I've already dealt with bullying on a scale Ron McCaughlin could only dream of. Everything else should be cheesecake, right? But this is different from Nathan. Punching, names, hatred—I've encountered it before from my brother, but this is a whole other beast. This is an assault on my identity, or at least a large part of it.

Maybe though . . . maybe if I remember I've handled the worst of what Nathan's thrown at me . . . maybe then I'll know I can handle Ron.

When we change in the locker room, Ron keeps quiet. Nobody talks to him, and he doesn't talk to anybody. At one point he looks at me, glares his meanest glare, but he doesn't say anything.

Maybe it's because Odin won't leave my side the whole time. Odin keeps his arms folded, staring Ron down from behind me. Eventually, Ron leaves, and it's just me and Odin in the locker room. "You didn't have to do that," I say.

"I hate bullies," Odin says. He sits on the bench.

"Well, thanks," I say. "Aren't you going to change?"

Odin's still not taking swimming, thanks to his totally not bogus "chlorine allergy," but he's started doing stuff with the eighth-grade gym class, and since the normal gym is next to the pool, Coach Streit told him to keep using this locker room. I've seen him wearing normal gym clothes. "I'm good," he says.

My turn to frown. "Don't want to change in front of the gay kid, huh?"

"That's not it," he says.

"Well, I'll leave," I say, "so you won't have to worry about it."

"Whatever, Colecuts."

Again with the food nicknames! "For someone who hates bullies, you sure like to pick on me a lot."

His eyes flare up, but he doesn't reply.

"Look, Odin," I say, "I don't want to fight with you. I don't hate you, even though you obviously hate me. I just . . . I just want you to know that."

"I don't hate you," Odin says without looking at me. "I'm getting into Gladstone and you're not, but that doesn't mean I hate you."

"Really?" I ask, ignoring the hot anger threatening to bubble over. "You could've fooled me."

Odin stands up from the bench and faces me, at my eye level. "You don't know me. Okay? So stop acting like you do."

"You're right. I don't. But I wish I did, so I could stop you from—" I almost say "from hurting." It almost slips out. I don't know why.

Odin's eyes narrow. "From what?"

"I don't know what your life is like or who you really are. All I know is I've learned everyone has their own problems. Sometimes you want to run and hide from them your whole life, but you can't run forever. And sometimes—"

"You don't know me, *okay*?"

"Sometimes you've got the courage you always needed all along."

Odin fumes. "This isn't a Hallmark card, you turd. You're so—so—"

"I believe in you." This also slips out. Why am I saying this? I *don't* believe in Odin. He's a jerk!

He goes silent.

"And—and swimming's not that bad, once you get the hang of it. At the start of the year I didn't know how to do anything except sink, but my friend helped me learn. You can do it too."

Like a car with a flat tire, Odin slowly lands back onto the bench. In a quiet voice, he says, "I know how to swim."

Huh? "Then why—"

"Hey, come on," Marcellus says from near the door. "We're about to start."

I want to tell Odin this isn't over, that I'm going to

follow up with him later, but . . . why should I? He's been nothing but rude to me. And he's my competition for Gladstone, so I shouldn't really be nice to him. It's him or me.

My eye throbs as I walk into the pool area, leaving Odin behind, unchanged.

I'm not looking forward to seeing Odin for social studies, but I get an unwelcome surprise at lunch: I get to see him at the Unstable Table first. Sitting, of course, in my seat.

"What are you doing?" I ask.

"Eating lunch," he says. "No assigned seats in the cafeteria."

My black eye pulsates. I take the empty seat next to where Zack sits, across from Madison and diagonal from Odin. "Hi, Odin," Zack says. "Madison, how's your salad? That kale looks pretty great."

"Mmrph," Madison garbles. He doesn't have any food in his mouth; he just sounds like that.

"Good!" Zack says. "That's really, really, really, really . . . really good."

This past week Madison's been more checked out than an overdue library book. His mind's clearly on Meredith Wood—they're always chatting in the hall, Madison blustering something incoherent and putting out his best deep "man voice" by lowering his normal voice a few octaves (or at least trying to). Zack has been trying his hardest to pretend he's not upset about the Madison situation, but in an obvious way, because Zack, champion of living an authentic life, is a bad actor and an even worse liar. Madison is annoyed because Zack is clearly not happy for Madison, and it's making Madison feel guilty about it (and also because Zack's lousy acting probably makes Madison feel like he's in a B-grade horror movie). And I'm still annoyed with them for not getting the June situation. Any time that's come up, they've clammed up about it, maybe because they recognize they can't say anything that won't irritate me worse than a rash. There have been no up-all-night hang-out-a-thons. Not even any regular hang-out-a-thons.

Odin showing up at the table is the absolute last thing I need. What do you say to a guy like him? You think he's doing something nice, but he's actually being a jerk. It's like he has no idea how to talk to people. It's like he doesn't even want to learn how! He's frustrating in every conceivable way. I even tried being nice to him, and he's still impossible! And now he's infecting my lunch period. Doesn't he care how he treats other people? Doesn't he—

"I said *get out of here*!"

There is commotion from behind me: the Stable Table. Where Connor sits. Connor and a bunch of jocks and—

And Ron.

Ron is gripping his lunch tray, about to sit down, but it looks like Connor is standing up, arms crossed, muscles squeezing out of his sleeves. "Get out of here!" Connor barks. "You're not welcome here anymore."

"What the heck?" Ron asks. "What's your problem?"

Connor barges forward at alarming speed. Ron looks like he wants to run, but the cafeteria is too crowded for him to make a break for it. "My problem"—Connor takes a step forward—"is with jerks"—another step—"like you"—step—"who beat up good guys"—he's right next to Ron, practically breathing down his neck—"like Alan!"

The massive cafeteria, housing all two hundred and fifty seventh graders, goes deathly silent. A teacher walks over. "Is there a problem, boys?"

Ron looks like he's either going to explode with rage or poop himself. Maybe both. "No problem," he forces out. "I was looking for somewhere else to sit."

He walks away.

"I recommend you have a seat, son," the teacher says to Connor.

But Connor's not done yet. Still standing, he looks at me—and gives me a big, big smile.

And Lord help me, my heart melts like it's baking in a waffle iron.

As Ron walks by, Odin glares at him and whispers under his breath, "Get lost, you bigot."

Then Zack does the most Zack thing in the world to do: he claps.

Then Madison slowly joins him.

Then, some tables down, Talia claps.

Eventually a few more people join in, leading to a light smattering of applause echoing around the cafeteria. It lasts for maybe ten seconds.

But it's enough.

As we all stop clapping, Zack wraps an arm around my shoulder and whispers, "You've got this."

And across the Unstable Table, Odin Thompson, who must think no one is looking, sheds a tear.

TEN

When I get home Monday, there are wings on the edges of my heart carrying me into the house. They carried me throughout Evergreen all day after lunch. I hope they'll never leave.

Then I get a call from June.

Great.

"Hello, sunshine," June cheerily says on the other end.

"Hi," I say. "I'm kind of busy right now."

"Oh yeah? What are you doing?"

"Not talking to you." The words surprise me, but she deserves them.

Instead of reacting like a typical human being, she laughs. "Oh ho! You're too funny, Alan. Listen, my dad wants us to hang out a bit before the dance. What do you say we do the mall tomorrow at four?"

"Oh uh, I've got to, uh, get six teeth pulled—"

"Great! See you then."

Click.

Ugh.

I set my phone down and . . . I don't think about June, at least for a while. I think about today at school, about kids standing up and clapping and Zack and Madison standing by me and Connor standing up for me and Odin crying (seriously, what?). I think, *He's no Nathan.* I think, *You've got this.*

Slowly, like I'm in a dream, I pull out my sketchbook.

Only the first page of this sketchbook is taken up with anything: my cretpoj. I've had false starts, but nothing I've committed to paper. Four weeks of no art. How have I survived?

I stare at the empty page, and, like I'm rediscovering how to be an artist after a century of dry spells, I begin.

The next day, Zack comes up to my locker before homeroom. "You should come over to my place this afternoon. Madison's invited too. My mom bought this special popcorn. It starts as kernels, but it pops in the microwave! It's amazing. You should come see it." He says in a smaller voice, "My mom's boyfriend might be over, but we can hang out in the kitchen or something, away from him. He smells like stale cabbage."

"Sorry, I can't," I say. "I've got plans."

"Plans?" Zack asks. "With who?"

"June. I got pressured into taking her to the mall. I'm not looking forward to it."

Zack stands there in silence.

"You, uh, okay?" I ask.

"I can come with you," he says. "I like the mall. They've got a flag store! It sells all these different flags. I found the Pennsylvania flag once and it was, like, two hundred feet wide."

"That would be cool," I say, "but I think June wants this to be a date."

"Even though you don't like girls."

"Zack—"

He picks at a strand of hair. "I don't get it. You were so proud of yourself for coming out. Is it because you got punched? You can't let one punch stand in the way of your dreams."

Easy for him to say. "It's not about that," I grumble. "We've been over this—"

"Madison!" Zack chirps as Madison approaches. "You should come over to my apartment after school. There's going to be popcorn. Wait until you see what kind!"

"Sorry," Madison says. He walks with his back upright, his shoulders out, a smile playing at his lips. "I'm hanging out with Meredith's friends."

Zack looks like Madison sent a spiked cannonball firing into his gut. "Oh."

I frown. "You're hanging out with Meredith's friends?"

"That's what I said." Madison walks past us into homeroom. "She told me there were other guys who asked her to the dance, but she said she was going with me instead. She turned down popular guys for me! Can you believe it?"

I walk behind him and whisper, "You see what this is doing to Zack, right?"

"Hmph." Madison crosses his arms. "Zack isn't my problem. He'll find a new girl to obsess over soon enough. If he was a good friend, he'd be happy for me." He narrows his eyes. "You're happy for me, right?"

I look down. "Yeah, I—I guess."

"You guess."

"I mean, yeah, I think it's great that you've found, you know, new friends and all."

He scowls and sits down. Behind me, Zack takes a seat and yells, "Well, that's okay, because I'm going to be hanging out with my new girlfriend. We can eat special popcorn together. We'll be so busy having fun, we can even ignore my mom's boyfriend."

"New girlfriend?" Rudy Brighton asks. "You?"

"That's right," Zack says with a grin.

This is getting out of control. My best friendships are falling apart at the seams, and I need to step in before it's too late. But how can I solve any problems when my friends keep acting so—so—unlike themselves?

"Must be nice having good friends," Odin says as I take my seat. How unusually nice of him. I wonder what the catch is.

I reply, "Yeah. They're cool." Normally.

"It sucks when people don't have friends," he says. His eyes are focused on his book.

Hmm. "Well, sometimes people have trouble finding friends after they move to a new school. They'll find kids they want to hang out with soon."

"Sometimes people didn't have any friends back home either."

Oh. "I didn't have friends until the beginning of middle school. It'll happen."

He flips a page in his book. "Sometimes people don't see anyone who'd make a good friend. Except one kid, but he might not like those people."

Uh. "There's some person I think could be a good friend for me too, but I don't think he likes me either."

"Well," he says, "that's a problem."

"Yeah."

He looks up from his book. We lock eyes for what feels like a million seconds.

Then I unleash a sneeze all over his face in all its snotty goodness.

A few kids laugh. I turn bright red. Odin, eyes squeezed shut, slowly wipes his cheek, where most of my mucus landed.

"Oh God," I whisper. "S-Sorry—"

Odin abruptly stands up and heads for the door.

"Odin, where are you going?" Miss Richter asks, taking roll. "You need to stay in your seat for morning announcements."

Either Odin doesn't hear her or he doesn't care, because he keeps walking until he leaves the room.

"Nice one, sneezelord," Rudy says. "Way to make the new kid feel welcome. He'll probably sic Thor on you now."

My legs are ready to sprint after Odin, but Miss Richter shakes her head at me. That's why I love Miss Richter: she can always tell what I'm thinking. Even if her answers to my questions aren't always what I want to hear.

In swimming Odin hovers by my side in the locker room; I don't know if he's actually protecting me from

Ron, but it's a nice gesture. When Ron leaves, Odin disappears into a bathroom stall to change. Is he hiding from me? Did I ruin whatever weird pseudo-friendship we were kind of building back in homeroom? Is it too late to salvage what could be a good thing?

It's been a long time since I doodled on a piece of paper. Almost all my art, including my very important post-cretpoj work, gets created in my sketchbook. I think, looking back, this was an unconscious decision when I was younger to make the jump from "little kid who doodles" to "serious artist."

But at the Unstable Table, I doodle on a piece of scrap paper. I spend so much time trying to focus on doing a good job that I barely touch my food.

"What are you doing?" Madison asks at one point.

"Drawing."

"Wow, you never draw in public," Zack says.

I shrug. Somehow this feels . . . different.

When we get to social studies, right after lunch, I take the doodle and leave it on the empty desk to my left.

Odin walks in the room and gets his materials out of his bag—and then he sees the doodle. He picks it up and examines it carefully.

I watch him out of the corner of my eye. His face

doesn't betray any emotion; it's like a blank canvas he hasn't painted on yet. He takes the drawing and puts it in his coat pocket.

Miss Richter starts class. Madison and Talia fight to answer questions first, Connor and Sheila keep staring at each other, Rudy acts obnoxious, Zack's eyes lock into unfocus. And next to me, Odin's pencil is hard at work at something that doesn't look like a class worksheet.

The bell rings. Odin gathers his stuff. Without making eye contact with me, he places the drawing he'd worked on all class on my desk, then walks out the room.

A little scribble of a dragon, breathing fire triumphantly into the air.

Just like mine.

I spend science class doodling another dragon. This one's flying. There are speed lines and everything. I have to do this in ten minutes before Mr. Masterson catches me and makes me go back to lab work, so it's not as polished as my other doodle masterpiece. In English class, I leave the drawing on Odin's desk, like I did in social studies.

He walks in and looks at it. He raises his eyebrows and sits down to work on sketching something else.

Right when the bell rings, he walks to my desk. My heart pounds, but I don't break eye contact. He stands there, unmoving, for the longest time, until we're the only people left in the room. He tosses the scribble onto my desk.

Then Odin does something I've never seen him do before. He smiles. It's not a big smile, not a cheek-to-cheek grin, not a smirk. It's a little, blink-and-you'll-miss-it upturn of his lips. He walks away before I can react.

His drawing is a rough sketch of a dragon with its arms crossed, glaring at the viewer. At me. A bulging vein pokes out of the dragon's head. But then I see the dragon's claws, with one thumb-like appendage sticking up to the sky, and I wonder if gym class isn't the only place you're allowed to change in middle school.

With my head held high, I walk to the bus circle. My mall rendezvous with June barely weighs on my mind. I made a friend today. I don't really get why Odin's friendship matters that much to me, given how jerkish he can be, but maybe there's goodness inside him that only needs sunlight to flourish. Maybe I need a friend right now, when Zack and Madison have proven unreliable, and Odin filled the void. Or maybe—

"Hey, Galan."

I jump three feet into the air as Ron lunges out from behind a tree in the bus circle. His hands are in his jacket pockets; his baseball cap is cocked slightly to the side. He can't attack me here, not with all these people around. Right?

"I said 'hey,'" he says. "It's rude to not say anything when someone says 'hey.'"

"What do you want?" I ask, sounding far braver than I feel. My eye pulsates.

Ron takes a step forward, and I immediately look for any adults or Connors nearby. No such luck. "I wanted to let you know something really important: you're dead. D-E-A-D. Dead."

I want to say, "I didn't know you knew how to spell," but I'd rather live to see the sunset, so I keep quiet.

Ron continues, "Because of you, my best friend kicked me out of our group. In front of the whole grade! I was humiliated. Now you're going to pay."

"How—how was that my fault? You're the one who—who hit me."

"Don't be stupid, Galan." He looks around. "I'll get you. When you don't expect it, I'll be there, ready to make your life hell." He spits at my feet and walks away.

Before he gets far, I call out, "Why?"

"Why what?"

"Why . . . do you hate me so much?"

He growls a bark of a growl, like he's gnawing on

jerky. Or a bone. “I don’t need a reason. I just hate little pussies like you. Watch your back, Galan—you’re going to really wish you hadn’t messed with me.”

I shiver in the chilly November air, and my eye threatens to swallow up the rest of my face into a black hole from which there is no escape. It’s going to take a lot of dragon doodles for me to see the light again.

ELEVEN

The Flower County Mall isn't crowded on a school night—honestly, it's barely crowded on weekends, let alone the middle of the week—but there are still clusters of teens hanging around, a few adults getting their watch batteries changed, a little girl throwing pennies into the fountain, and at least six mall walkers decked out in spandex. A good small crowd for what will hopefully be a not-too-terrible evening. I could use a break.

I wait by the entrance to a department store for a few minutes before June Harrison comes sauntering across the shiny floor like she owns the place. "Hello, Mr. Cole," she says.

"Hi."

"No, no, you're supposed to say, 'Hello, Ms. Harrison.'

It's one of the rules of banter."

"Okay."

"What happened to your face?"

I shove my hands into my pocket. "I got sucked into a black hole."

"That must've hurt."

"No more than what my dad did to me after that company dinner."

"All right, all right, I get it. What do you want from me?"

"I don't know. Maybe an apology?" I'm getting loud. The little girl at the fountain looks at us and winds up dropping a penny onto the floor.

June sighs theatrically. "I tried helping you, Alan. If you didn't see people as fundamentally bad before that dinner, I'm sure you do now."

"No, I don't."

She raises an eyebrow. "How'd you really get that black eye?"

My turn to sigh, but mine's a real one. "So what do you want to do? Do you need to buy something?"

"Buy something? Nobody comes to the mall to buy something. You come to the mall to hang out."

We walk down the corridors, passing clothing stores, a Starbucks, and a tanning salon. As we move past storefronts, I say, "I guess we're supposed to talk and become friends so it isn't weird that we're going to the dance together even though we hate each other."

"You hate me?" June asks. She sounds surprised.

"No. But you hate me." This conversation sounds similar to one from earlier in the day.

"I don't hate you, Alan. I like you. I think you and I have potential as rivals. Superhero and supervillain! I'll commit crimes, and you try to save the day, and we can have philosophical battles all the time about the nature of humanity, and—"

"*Stop!*"

My voice echoes down the open mall. "Just stop it, okay? Forget all the weird stuff about being a bad guy and people being bad and all of that. Can you . . . act like a real human being? Please?"

June's face is blank. "Do you know why I wanted to talk to you at the company dinner?"

I shake my head.

"Part of it was that your dad made fun of you for your art, and I wanted to find out more about you. Part of it was how you looked—a combination of scared and bored. I know that combination all too well. But the biggest part was simply that you were the only other kid my age there. And I was bored. And I wanted to mess with someone. I meant what I said about people being bad, especially me.

"But you . . . when you stopped me from putting that dead rat in the punch, you flew in the face of that. I don't know many good people. I can probably count them on one hand! You're an oddity. I want to keep you in a zoo and study you. An authentic good person. The rarest of species.

"You, Alan Cole, are a good person. I, June Harrison, am a bad person. And I . . . I'm sorry for contaminating you."

June studies the floor.

"It's not that simple," I say. "Everyone has good and bad in them. Even me. Even you." Even Odin. Even Madison. Even *Zack*.

She takes a deep breath. "Anyway, there you have it. I've exposed my fragile innards to you. I've never done that to anyone before. You should feel very honored."

Something passes between us, a gust of wind that ruffles my hair. "Okay," I say.

"Okay?"

"Okay."

June gestures down the corridor. "Shall we?"

I nod.

We take three steps toward a sporting goods store and Ron walks out.

I freeze dead in my tracks. D-E-A-D in my tracks. Ron stops too.

June walks a few paces, then sees me stopped. "Coming?"

Then I notice someone by Ron's side: a little boy, maybe seven or eight years old. He's wearing a baseball cap perched at the same angle as Ron's. "Come on, Ronnie!" he squeaks. "You said you'd carry me!"

"In a minute," Ron says.

I swallow, and that seems to regain control of my mouth. "Let's walk on the other side," I say.

June, always observant, seems to put the pieces together quickly. She crosses her arms. "Hello," she says. "Fine day to browse sporting goods, isn't it?"

"Ronnie!" the little boy yelps. "Are these your friends from school?"

Ron's lip curls. "No. They're not my friends. I don't—"

"I'm Aaron!" The boy bounds over to June and shakes her hand.

She smirks. "Nice to meet you."

Aaron bounces to me and extends his hand. Ron looks like he's about to erupt like Pompeii, but I shake the kid's hand anyway.

"What are your names?" Aaron asks.

"You can call me June," my mall walking companion says.

"Uh," I say, looking again at Ron, who's now squeezed his hands into fists. "Alan."

"Alan!" Aaron squeals. "That starts with *A*! Like my name!"

I chuckle nervously. "Uh, yeah. Our names both end with *N* too."

Aaron looks like he just got told Santa is coming a month early, and all the presents on his sleigh are for him. "Ronnie! Alan and me have the same name basically!" He turns back to me and flashes a gap-toothed grin. "Let's be friends!"

"Uh . . ." Now Ron is walking over to us.

"You can come over, and we can play freeze tag!" Aaron chirps. He taps my leg. "Tag! You're frozen!"

"Let's go," Ron says.

"Awwwww, I want to stay and play with Alan!"

"You don't want to play with Alan. He'll mess you up."

Aaron looks at me, squinting like he's trying to believe his big brother's words. "Really?"

"Yeah. Alan's a pussy."

Aaron nods sagely. "Okay. Bye, pussy!"

The McCaughlin brothers start to walk away, but—

"Hold it," June says. "I'm sorry, but I'm not clear on something."

"Great," Ron says. "Keep being not clear. I'm going to keep walking."

"Why would Alan 'mess up' your brother?"

Aaron looks up at Ron.

"I'm not going to say it in front of him," Ron growls.

Oh no oh no oh no June doesn't know I'm gay, if she finds out she could tell her dad and her dad might tell my dad oh no oh no oh no—

"What is it?" Aaron asks. "Is it 'cause he got a Dalmatian eye?"

"It's disgusting," Ron spits. "It's not something you talk about with little kids."

"There's nothing *wrong* with it," I say, like a Pop-Tart about to explode in the microwave.

"Don't you dare," Ron says.

I look at June the mask, at Ron the furious, at Aaron the curious. I make my decision. "I'm gay," I say to Aaron. "It means I get crushes on other boys and not on girls. And there's nothing wrong with it." I face Ron. "At all."

"Oh," Aaron says. "Cool!"

"No it is not cool!" Ron yells. "Being gay is terrible!"

"Why, Ronnie? Isn't Daddy gay?"

Wait. What?

"That's why it's terrible," Ron says through a clenched jaw. "It means you're not a real man. Like Dad."

"Oh please," June says. "Is that why you punched Alan in the face? Because you're a real man, and he's not?"

Ron throws his hands into the air. "Come on, Aaron. We're leaving."

"Did you punch Alan, Ronnie? Did you really?"

"And 'pussy' is a really bad thing to call someone, Aaron," June says. "If you're going to use an insult, get creative."

Ron scoops up Aaron and places him on his shoulders. He sears his eyeballs through my face.

"Okay!" Aaron cries. "Bye, fartbutts!"

"Better!" June calls back.

The McCaughlins walk past us and into another store. My black eye trembles but doesn't throb. I might have just made things colossally worse between me and Ron, but . . . I don't feel all that bad about it. And what the heck did Aaron mean—is their dad actually—

"Gay, huh?" June asks.

Crap. "Please don't tell my dad," I whisper.

"Why shouldn't I?"

"I-I—" I frantically look at the sporting goods store. "I'll buy you a life vest?"

She cracks up. "A life vest? Really?"

Oh God.

"How did you know that's what I always wanted?"

"I . . . I just knew."

She smiles. "Let's go in the thrift store. We can see if they have any off-brand stuffed animals. Last time I was here I bought Large Bird and Smelmo."

We make our way down the corridor. "Hey, June?"

"Yes?"

"Thanks for—"

"Shh." She places a finger on my lips. "Of course, you know what this means."

"You're not a totally bad person after all?"

"What? No, I meant I can't go to the dance with you."

"You—huh?"

"Wouldn't you rather go with a boy?"

"I mean . . . I guess . . . but my dad—"

"Leave it to me. I'll take care of everything."

My head is spinning. So I won't have to go to the dance with June anymore? And Dad could possibly be okay with that? "June, I-I—"

"No trouble at all," she says. "After all, what are friends for?"

TWELVE

Wednesday morning I walk into homeroom and there's a folded piece of paper on my desk. Heart racing, I unfold it to see a big, black dragon, steam coming out of its nostrils. Odin, next to me, reads a book.

"I thought it was my turn," I say.

"Do you have anything?" he asks.

My cheeks get hot. After I did my homework I was out with June. "No, but—"

"Good thing I came prepared, huh?" He turns the page to his book, careful not to touch all the papers carefully laid out on his desk.

I look at the doodle again. "Black dragon. You're mixing it up."

"Dragons come in lots of colors."

Zack hasn't arrived in homeroom yet. Neither has Madison. I open my backpack to place the scribble in my notebook, but my elbow slips off my desk and everything clatters to the floor.

"Wow, tough break, man," Rudy says. He doesn't lift a finger to help me pick up my stuff. Neither does anyone else—the only other two kids who might are Connor and Talia, and Connor's busy looking at his phone with Sheila and engaging in some pretty sloppy PDA, and Talia is studying homework. So it falls on me to pick up my notebooks, papers, pencils, and sketchb—

Oh crap.

Oh. Crap.

My sketchbook's fallen open right in front of Odin's desk.

To the second page.

The page that's got my post-cretpoj work on it.

The work that's—that's—

Odin looks up from his book.

I am frozen. Powerless.

He grabs my sketchbook.

His jaw drops.

I try swallowing, but I can't work the muscle.

Finally, after what feels like an endless eternity of Odin staring, *staring* at my sketchbook, he sets it down.

Then he slowly looks up at me.

"That's me," he says.

I'd nod, but my neck is locked into place.

"You're sketching me."

It's only at this point do I realize that, yes, that's exactly what I'd been doing. Sketching Odin with the intent of painting him, like I did with my cretpoj. I'd been denying that ever since I started. Why was I denying that? I try coughing to regain my voice. It works. Sort of. "Y-Yeah. I am. Was. I w-was."

Odin keeps staring at me, but it's not a stare of hatred. It's a stare of . . . curiosity? Whatever it is, I try to ignore it as I pick up the rest of my things. After loading my school day into my bag, I check back in with Odin—

—and he's flipped the page. He's looking at my cretpoj.

He's looking at my cretpoj!

I make a gurgling sound that's a cross between a screaming newborn and a dying beaver and actually lunge for the book. I mean *lunge*—I throw my whole body into it so hard that Odin's desk shrieks on the linoleum, and then the desk goes crashing to the floor, complete with me—and Odin—inside it.

Ow.

It takes me a few seconds to take stock of my surroundings from my prone position on the floor.

"Boys!" Miss Richter cries.

All of homeroom has gathered round to observe the desk crash, including Madison and Zack, who have made sudden appearances from somewhere along the space-time continuum. I'm about to sit up, when Odin shoves me off him onto the floor.

"Are either of you hurt?" Miss Richter asks, getting both of us to our feet.

Odin grumbles something noncommittal, picking up his book and making sure none of the page corners are creased.

"I'm, uh, fine," I say. My cheeks feel like they're in the middle of a Bunsen burner. Now other kids have started to laugh and whisper (or in Rudy's case, yell). Once Miss Richter gets everybody sorted out and makes sure neither of us has any internal bleeding, we've talked through almost the entire morning announcements.

I can't even look at Odin. What came over me? Am I that obsessive about people not seeing my cretpoj that I act like an animal? What is *wrong* with me? I bury my head in my hands for the rest of homeroom.

Once we line up to leave, something pokes my arm: my sketchbook. Odin nudges me with the edge of a page, but he gets up to leave before I can apologize. Boy, if it's not sneezing on his face, it's this. If he didn't hate me before, he must really hate me now.

Zack and Madison try to get my attention as we leave, but it's Miss Richter who beckons me over first. "I have to say, I'm disappointed in you," my favorite teacher says, and that stings almost as much as a punch in the face. "What were you thinking?"

"I don't know," I say. "I—I lost it."

"I know that much. I'm going to have to give you a detention. Odin could have gotten seriously hurt. So could you. I don't know what you were trying to do, but whatever it was, it's not worth it. Okay?"

I nod, looking at the floor.

I leave homeroom with my head about as low as it can go while still allowing me to walk upright. Not only does Odin know I was sketching him—I'm still not sure why I'm so embarrassed by that—he saw my cretpoj, and I fell into some kind of trance and probably humiliated him, and for all I know he could have scraped his elbow or broken his hip, and—and—

"You're ridiculous, you know that?" Odin says, walking behind me.

I yelp a very high-pitched yelp. "Uh, h-hi. Sorry about, uh, before—"

"Your art's not bad," he says.

My heart swells so big it threatens to burst out of my rib cage.

"I'm still getting into Gladstone instead of you," Odin says. "But your stuff isn't bad."

I breathe a sigh of relief. He doesn't sound mad. Well, no madder than normal. "Thanks."

"Your sketching is off, but your painting is good," Odin continues as we walk down the hall to swimming class. "Your self-portrait was way better than . . . the other one."

My cheeks flare up again.

"You should give it to the class president," Odin says as we arrive at the pool area. "She'd love to hang that up."

"I can't," I say.

"Why?"

"It's . . ." I hesitate, unsure of how to phrase this. "It's really personal. It's like, if I show it to other people, they'll be able to look in my . . . in my soul."

Odin frowns. "So? You've got a good soul. You shouldn't mind showing it off." He stares at me for a few seconds, and then he walks into the locker room.

I linger outside the gym area for a few moments, mulling over Odin's words. I've got a good soul, huh? Says the guy I just humiliated and who's been mostly jerkish to me since he arrived. We haven't exactly been chummy. What does Odin Thompson know about my soul?

* * *

At lunch I manage to catch up to Talia in line. I tap her on the shoulder.

"Alan Cole," she says. "I'm glad you're getting my attention more gently than slamming into me with your shoulder."

"Forget about that," I say. "I've got something for you." I put my empty tray under my arm and very carefully—not taking any chances after this morning—take out a sheet of paper.

Talia's eyes narrow. "What's this? If it's a proposal for a new club, you need to fill out form 21-B on the Evergreen website before it can be looked at by—" She adjusts her glasses. "Oh my. Is this what I think it is?"

"It's a photocopy," I say, "but yeah."

We move up in line. Talia takes the photocretpoj and studies it. Sweat builds on my back as I study her face. "Yes, this will do nicely," she finally says, placing it in her backpack.

We move up in line a few more times before I get the courage to ask, "So, uh, what did you think?"

"Hm? What did I think of what?"

"Of my, uh, cretpoj."

"Oh. It's good. It looks just like you. I'm no art critic, but you really captured . . . yourself." She nods, apparently pleased with that answer. "I think the school will be delighted to learn where you came from."

"Thanks."

We move up in line. "Alan Cole," Talia says, facing away from me. "I'd like to ask you something personal."

Uh-oh. "Okay."

"What do you do when . . . you want something you can never have?"

I think of Connor and Sheila playing tongue hockey every chance they can get, and I grip the edges of my lunch tray. "Nothing. You can't do anything. And it sucks."

Talia's shoulders droop a little. "I see. I'm asking for a friend, of course."

Now, I know that's a lie, because Talia MacDonald doesn't have any friends. "Well," I say, "I guess all you can do is keep your head up and try your best to move on."

Talia doesn't say anything at first as we approach the lunch stations. Eventually she says, "It's hard though, isn't it? When you want the world to be something it isn't. You thought becoming Sapling class president would help you solve all the problems in the school, but there are still problems everywhere, all the time. Bullying and hardship and oppression. The world is . . . challenging. At least my friend says it is."

I sigh. "Yeah. It's hard. But you need to focus on what

you can change now and move on from what you can't. If you're stuck in the past, you can't look toward the future. I mean, that's what they say in the movies."

Talia takes a helping of creamed corn and looks back at me. "You're right. Change what I can, move on from what I can't, then look toward the future. Good advice. For my friend." She takes a deep breath, and, like it's some butt-clenching effort—which, for Talia, it is—she says, "Thanks."

As I walk toward the Unstable Table I pass by the Stable Table, where Connor entertains his Ron-less table of jocks (and now Sheila), and he gives her a big smile, and I think, Alan Cole, it's time to move on. Connor Garcia is not interested in you, and he will never be interested in you, and *you are going to have to deal with it.* If he smiles at you or laughs at a joke of yours or even stands up for you to a bully, he's doing so as a friend, not because he *likes* you the way you like him. Connor is straight and you are gay and that's never going to change.

Okay?

You are twelve years old and that is too young to worry about a broken heart.

"Are you okay?" Zack asks as I sit down. "You look distracted."

I shake my head. "Don't worry about it. Just trying to remember something."

Connor's laugh bounces through the air, landing squarely inside my eardrums, and I try to let it pass right on by, floating along the musty cafeteria air, dissolving into the surrounding noise.

THIRTEEN

Lab days in ASPEN science class are normally free-for-alls. Mr. Masterson tells us to work on experiments with our lab partners, and he barely comes around to check on our progress, so it's largely a period where we can chitchat. And when your lab partners are Madison and Zack, that's a recipe for fun.

At least it used to be.

This past week we've worked mostly in silence, though Zack's certainly tried his darnedest to loosen things up. Last Friday he kept asking us to play "Name That Tune," but he's terrible at whistling, so all he really did was spit on our worksheets. Madison's been so distracted, probably thinking about Meredith, that he keeps making easy mistakes in the lab—something normally unheard of.

And I . . . I've got a lot on my mind too.

"Hey, guys," Zack says as I look through the microscope at some amoebas (or maybe that's amoebae), "you should come over after school. I've got plenty of special popcorn."

"Oh, I can't," Madison says, flipping aimlessly through notes. "I'm going to the mall with Meredith and her friends."

"The mall," Zack mutters. "Malls are dying, Madison. Did you know that? Did *you* know that, Alan? Maybe if you knew that you wouldn't have gone there with June yesterday."

I really don't want to get into things with Zack right now, so I keep my eye focused on the amoebae (or is that amoebas?) writhing under the microscope slide.

"The mall is a fine place to hang out with friends," Madison says.

"But I'm your friend," Zack says. "And I've got special popcorn. And my mom's horrible boyfriend will be there, so we can make fun of his mustache together."

That stops me. Zack does not make fun of people. Is this part of why he's been so spacey (even for him) lately? Mom-dating woes?

"What do your parents think of Meredith?" I ask Madison to change the subject.

Madison runs a hand over his hair. "Er, I . . . might not . . . have told them yet."

"Huh?" I can't have heard him right. "Wasn't the whole reason you wanted a date so your parents could see you didn't need to lose all this weight?"

"No, that was the reason *Zack* wanted me to get a date."

Zack is oddly quiet, staring through the whiteboard at the front of the room.

"Then why haven't you told them?"

Madison frowns, still scouring his notes for information that may or may not be there. "I don't know. I suppose I'm worried they'll ruin it. You know how they are."

I picture Bob and Dorothy Truman, their fake smiles and stifling, backhanded encouragement, and I shudder. "Maybe you're right. But you can't keep it a secret forever."

We go back to working in silence. Madison fills out whatever worksheet he was looking for, I log data on the amoebasasae, and Zack says, in a voice that sounds like it's an inch away from shattering, "I'm happy for you, Madison. Really. My girlfriend Hepzibah is too."

"Mm," Madison grunts. "That's nice."

And I don't know what comes over me, but I reach out to Madison's notebook, and I rip the page he's working on out.

"Hey!" he gasps. "What are you—"

"You're embarrassed by us," I whisper. "You think we're not worth hanging out with anymore. Is that it?"

He snatches the torn paper from my hand. "Do you remember how we always used to call ourselves losers? As some sort of symbol of pride?"

I nod.

"I got tired of being a loser."

I think of Dad calling me a loser. It sounds so different coming from him than it does from my friends. Madison rejecting the label we reclaimed from society makes me want to puke out of my eye sockets. "Do you even like Meredith?"

He chuckles. "What kind of question is that? Obviously I like her. I wouldn't be spending so much time with her if I didn't."

"It seems like you're into Meredith because . . . she's the first girl who's been into you."

Madison frowns. "What are you implying?"

"You're really going out of your way to hang out with someone you don't care about."

My friend shakes his head. "That's very hypocritical of you."

"Huh?"

"Hypocritical. Acting as if you have a higher standard than you—"

"I know what hypocritical means. I don't see how I'm—"

"You don't see it?" Madison asks. "You don't see how I'm not the only one going to the dance with someone I might not be madly in love with but who provides . . . certain benefits? You really have the gall to criticize me for how I behave with Meredith, but the way you act with June Harrison is so much better? You took her to the mall yesterday. On a date!"

I turn bright red. "Weren't you the one who wanted me to 'try out girls'?"

"Of course I was. But it's clear you don't like her. So don't criticize how I act when you're doing the same thing!"

The room is silent. I didn't realize how loud we were. "Boys, please focus on your lab," Mr. Masterson says.

"I'm probably not even going to the stupid dance with June anymore," I whisper. "So forget it."

Odin looks at me from his own lab table, then quickly looks back down.

"You know," Madison whispers, "this was exactly what Meredith said."

"Wait, what?"

"She said you would be jealous of me. It's clear she was right."

"Jealous?" I cry. "I'm not—"

"You're both jealous of my success with Meredith. Isn't it obvious?"

"Oh yeah, of course I'm jealous," I say. "That's one less girl I get to try out."

Madison's eyes narrow.

"Guys, hang on," Zack pleads, coming back to life. "Nobody's jealous of you, Madison. We miss you, that's all. We liked you better when you were a loser like us."

"I'm through being a loser," Madison says.

"Could've fooled me." The words tear out of me, pulled up from some deep abyss by a black magnet dredging up toxins. I fight back the hot pressure behind my eyes. Why did I say that? Why did I make a bad situation even worse? A worse situation unsalvageable?

Madison's face scrunches up. "I thought you of all people would understand. When you've been picked on your whole life for something, to get attention from someone you thought would never look at you for two seconds, that's incredible. I like Meredith. And I'm going to do whatever I can to be her friend—and maybe even something more! Don't you understand that? Don't you understand what it's like to be—"

He abruptly halts as we all realize once again how loud we are and how public our fight has become. Everyone in the room is looking at us. "Forget it," Madison spits.

"Fine," I spit, "it's forgotten."

"Fine," Zack spits, "me and Hepzibah will have all the special popcorn to ourselves."

Fine. Fine fine fine.

Everything is fine.

Fine.

Fine.

Fine.

I stomp and crash around Evergreen aimlessly, kind of making my way to English but not really, when someone says, "Hey."

I almost snap at whoever it is. But it's Odin. Glad I didn't. "Hi," I say.

"I was thinking about your art," he says, walking alongside me.

"Yeah?"

"Your sketching still sucks."

It's like he shoves a bicycle spoke in my heart. That is not what I need to hear right now. "Oh yeah?" I say loudly. "Then why don't you do it yourself?"

Odin stops walking. "Sure. Why not? I'll sketch, and you paint. Come over after school."

I bump into a very large teacher and almost get

knocked off my feet. "Uh, s-sure. Okay. I guess that works."

"Good. Follow me to the bus circle after English, and we'll take my bus home. Don't be late. I'll leave without you if you're not there."

"O-Okay. I might have to go home to do my homework first."

"Then here's my phone number. Text me when you're on your way."

He gives me his number, and I give him mine. We walk in silence the rest of the way to English, but I like this silence. It's a silence of possibility, a silence that almost makes me forget how I just had an absolute mess of an argument with my two best friends, a silence that makes my regrets softer around the edges, a silence that makes me feel a little less alone. I'm actually going over to Odin's house. Odin Thompson, the guy who's been both a huge jerk and a . . . slightly less huge jerk to me. Odin, my Gladstone competition. What am I thinking? Why does he even want to hang out with me if he dislikes me so much? Why does he want to do art with me, of all people?

And why can't I wait to find out?

When we reach Mrs. Ront's room, I stop off at the water fountain, head buzzing, when I hear, "Hey, Galan."

Oh no.

"Surprised to see me?" Ron growls. "You really messed up my little brother yesterday. You have any idea how much he kept talking about you? It was disgusting. Plus, Connor turned all my friends against me, and that's your fault too."

There's a teacher just behind Ron, so I know I'll be safe, at least until the bell rings. But after that?

"Now it's payback time," he sneers. "Meet me in the grove by the cafeteria after school, and I'll make good on that death sentence."

I look at the nearby teacher. "What if I . . . don't show up?"

"Then maybe I'll beat up your swimming bodyguard instead. Or maybe I'll go for one of your other friends—Fatison or the weirdo with the messy hair. They'll get their faces kicked in, all because you ran away like a pussy."

Oh God.

He's no Nathan.

The whole reason I never had friends when Nathan was at his worst was because he would target them to "punish" me. Now Ron is doing the same thing. What choice do I have?

"I'll be there," I say in a very, very quiet voice.

"Good." Ron walks off. "Don't be late."

I've got two very different meetups with two very different people scheduled for today, and I've got a feeling one's going to be much, much worse.

FOURTEEN

When English class ends, I quickly dart down the hall, away from anyone who might be able to tell what's about to happen. I take a few deep breaths to steady myself. This is like willingly walking into a jungle wearing a poncho made of raw meat. But I've got to protect my friends.

Ron is exiting his last class, and I dash past him; I'll see him soon enough. I look behind me to see if he's following me—and something weird happens. Ron stops at a water fountain, and Connor walks toward him and thuds his shoulder into Ron's side, practically knocking Ron over. Water spurts from Ron's mouth like a bullet. Connor keeps walking, heading down another hall; it doesn't look like he even notices me. Ron tries to recover quickly, but he shakes a little as he walks off.

Maybe Connor wasn't watching where he was going? Or maybe Connor was just goofing around? I guess it doesn't matter—someone like Ron deserves to be picked on.

Right?

I've never been to this little wooded area behind the cafeteria. I can see why Ron picked it—stand just behind the cluster of bushes, and nobody can see a thing. Nobody can see my blood, about to be coating Ron's fists; nobody can see my teeth, plucked out to make Ron's necklace. My black eye is screaming like it hasn't in a week—it's ready to welcome its new neighbor.

Ron's hunched beside a bush as I approach, with my legs heavy and my feet tied down with rocks. As I get closer, I notice he's sniffing a flower. That's about the last thing I expected Ron McCaughlin to be doing before he takes a nuclear bomb to my rib cage. What's next, reciting poetry?

He stands up and looks at me. There's no sign of Connor's shoulder assault—he's tough, confident, ready. "Least you know when you can't run away. Nobody here to protect you this time."

All English class I tried to think of ways I could get out of this and still save my friends. None of them were good. But I'll try anything.

"Any last words?"

Here goes nothing. "Y-You know, you can't beat me up again. Everyone will know you did it. Then you might get something worse than a suspension."

"I'll hit you where it won't leave a mark." He takes a step forward.

Ah, the old Nathan tactic. Keep going, Alan. "You'll, uh, you could hurt yourself. You're a star player on the soccer team. Kick me the wrong way, and it could really mess up your A-game."

"Soccer season's over." Another step forward.

I could run. I could run to the bus circle and hide and never look back. Until he hurts my friends. "It's not, uh, it's not s-satisfying to, uh, beat me up like this, wouldn't you, uh, wouldn't you rather do it with other people around, so you c-can, uh, so you c-can—"

He's right in front of me.

I whisper, "Does your brother know you're a bully?"

He grips me by the shirt. "Don't you *dare* bring Aaron into this."

"Aaron's a good kid," I ramble, I stammer, not even aware of what comes out of my mouth, "and he really looks up to you, and if he knew you went around beating up other kids, what kind of message is that sending, he's so young, he loves you—"

His grip shakes, sends ripples through my body. "Shut *up*."

"—and he doesn't care if I'm gay, Ron! Why should you?"

"Shut *up*, shut *up*, shut *up*!" He screams the last word in my face. "He's my brother, not yours, you gay piece of trash! The last thing I want is for him to turn out like you! It's my freaking job to protect him from garbage!"

Words thunder up from my throat, I can't stop them, they bark at Ron and collide off his face—"I am *not* garbage."

"That's just what my dad said," Ron growls. "Right after he left us. For a *man*."

Whoa.

He shakes me back and forth, still clutching my shirt. "My dad's a freaking homo! And he ran away from us. From *me*. That's why I never run away. Not from a fight, not from other homos like you who keep trying to get in my way. Not from anybody."

"I didn't see you push Connor back at the water fountain."

Oh God I wish I didn't say that, but I am beyond the point of rational response, I am on full alert—

His eyes flicker. His nostrils flare. For a brief second, he looks scared. Not scared of Connor—scared I saw his "weakness." "You," he screams, "you—you—"

My body shakes, but I somehow squeeze free from Ron's grasp. Something tells me the fight is over. Something tells me Ron "lost." Something tells me—

A bomber jet collides with my stomach, and I'm on the grass, wheezing and clutching my body like something detonated next to my appendix.

Something tells me I was wrong.

Ron stands above me and cracks his knuckles. I can feel the searing hatred from his eyes scalding me. "You really got some nerve, homo," he whispers. "You think I'm just going to roll over and take your crap? You've got another thing coming."

I groan.

He rolls me over and looks me square in the eyes. "So listen up: mention my brother again, or mention Connor again, and I'll rip your arms off and shove them down your throat. You haven't even seen me mad yet."

"Not . . . my . . . fault . . ."

He kicks me in the ribs. "Just wait," he says. "Next time's going to be even worse. You're going to really regret taking away my friends and messing with my family."

"Didn't . . . do . . . anything . . ."

Another kick, this one blocked by my arms. He's not paying attention. He's lashing out aimlessly, like he's just going through the motions, like his heart isn't even in it. Or is that wishful thinking?

He spits on me, walks over my prone body, and leaves.

And I lie there, shaking and groaning, in the grass.

FIFTEEN

I'm silent when Mom picks me up half an hour later. The heat from the car blasts my face, and I close my eyes, pretending I'm hibernating deep in a cave, where nobody can find me.

"Is everything okay?" Mom asks when we stop at a light.

"Yeah." My voice sounds like I haven't used it in four hundred years. "Everything's fine."

Mom studies me. I give her a thumbs-up and go back to closing my eyes.

I wonder what Zack and Madison are doing right now. If Zack's eating his "special popcorn." If Madison's off to the mall with his new friends. I wonder if they're worried about me and Ron, if they've spared a thought for my safety and well-being.

I wonder if they'd take a punch to the gut for me anymore.

As the light changes, my phone chimes: a text. From Odin. All it says is:

Hello

I go to text back, but another comes in:

It's Odin

Then three more:

Odin Thompson

From school

We have class together

By now I'm smiling. I thought I'd never smile again after being Ron's pincushion, but there you have it. "Hey Mom," I say, "can you drop me off at a friend's house?"

When I ring the doorbell at a townhome, Odin answers the door. "Take your shoes off," he says.

Odin's home is smaller than mine—cozier, you might say—and there are unpacked moving boxes all over the living room. We walk past a glass desk. I stop to pick up the picture frame next to the computer monitor: it's a younger Odin on the shoulders of a man who has his short, curly hair. Odin is smiling.

Wow.

I didn't think Odin knew how to smile like that.

"Come on," he says impatiently, and I set the picture down.

We walk upstairs to Odin's room. It's cozier than my room in every respect: smaller bed, smaller dresser, smaller closet. It's not microscopic like Zack's apartment room though. It's also meticulously clean: no stray socks clog up the floor; the sheets and covers on his bed look like they belong in a catalog; even his stacks and stacks of books, encompassing what looks like every topic under the sun, are alphabetized by author.

"Let me see your sketchbook," he says, snapping me out of observational mode.

I hesitate.

He rolls his eyes. "You've got two things in there, and I've seen them both already. Let me see it."

I hand him my sketchbook. He's gentle with his touch, taking great care to not crease the firm, thick, chalky pages. He stares at my cretpoj for a while, then at the outline of his own face. He flips back and forth between the pages a few times. I try to occupy myself with something else to take my mind off the lingering pain in my stomach and arms, and the flashes of Ron calling me garbage that sear like I'm on a skillet, so I say, "Can I see yours?"

He hands me a blue sketchbook without taking his eyes off mine.

I browse Odin's art, expecting to see dragons, dragons, and more dragons. And there are a few snapshots of dragon life throughout the pages, but a lot of it is close-ups of faces. Plenty of them. They're less realistic than mine, with more exaggerated facial features and expressions. But they're incredibly evocative. I flip through his sketches, full of people I don't recognize. Eventually I reach the end of the book and—

Oh.

Staring back at me behind strands of parted hair is a very detailed sketch of my face, rivaling my cretpoj when it comes to accuracy. There's a heavy red blush around its cheeks and deep, soulful eyes full of strength and power. It's me. He—he drew me.

"Okay," Odin says. "I figured out your problem."

I don't respond. I can't take my eyes off myself.

"Your problem is you're sketching too fast. You clearly want to get to the painting and don't want to take the time to do a decent job on the sketch. So when you—hey! You listening?" He wheels his desk chair to me and snatches his sketchbook out of my hands. Then he sees what I'm looking at.

"It, uh, looks nice," I squeak.

Odin sets his book aside. "Just returning the favor," he says quietly.

"Yeah. Of course."

"Anyway, your paint work is solid. Great blending of colors, great brush strokes. But if you don't build from a solid foundation, it's going to come out sloppy." He grabs a stray piece of parchment paper and hands it to me. "Paint this."

I look at the drawing: a girl's happy, smiling face. "I can't paint over something you drew."

"It's all right," he says. "I can make more." He sets an egg timer on his desk. "Go."

My body tenses up. "I can't paint on a timer."

"Sure you can," he says. "And you better hurry up, because you wasted ten seconds."

I grumble, but I take my brush to his sketch.

We work in silence. He draws something new, I paint over something old. It's a weird feeling painting over someone else's line work, but I eventually get into a comfortable rhythm, finding my own details to emphasize, my own pauses to lay into the page. Right when I put the finishing touches on the girl's chin, the egg timer chimes.

"Show me," Odin says.

I hold up the painting. Odin studies it.

"I think it turned out pretty good," I say. "I've never done anything like this before."

Odin nods. "It looks a lot better than what you were doing before."

"Well, I wouldn't say it looks *better*—"

"I drew this now," Odin says, handing me a picture of an anthropomorphic fox, looking up at the sky. "I tried making it more like your style."

"I've, uh, never drawn foxes before."

"You know what I mean." He resets the egg timer. "Go."

Three hours later, we've gotten six fully painted pictures out of the deal.

Odin rotates his wrist. "How do you feel?"

I look over all these paintings, pieces of art I made with someone. "I have to admit, they do look pretty great." About an hour ago, I said I wanted to do some sketching, and Odin could do some painting. So we switched. The results weren't nearly as good, but it was nice to mix it up. Ron's beating still floats around the back of my head, but it hasn't poked its way to the front, though my stomach still hurts when I shift on Odin's bed. A few times during the artfest I caught Odin looking at me, but when I would look at him, his eyes would drop back to his sketchbook. He probably wanted to make sure I was staying on task and not doodling a ladybug on the windowsill or something.

Odin stands up and stretches. "I haven't gotten this much art done in . . . a long time."

"Yeah," I say. "Maybe next time we can spend longer on one individual painting instead of rushing through a bunch. I mean, I still had fun doing this, but—"

"Nah," Odin interrupts. I expect him to disagree, but instead he says, "We can try different things. I like getting lots of art done fast, but your stuff tends to be more detailed. You don't take shortcuts."

I blush. "I, uh, thanks. Hey, Odin, can I tell you a secret?"

He immediately sits back down and listens.

"My cretpoj, I mean, my self-portrait, I always thought it would, well—that it would change the world."

Odin looks disappointed. "Art doesn't change the world," he says. "Artists do."

"What's the difference?"

"Art is a tool for an artist to express themselves. It's only as strong as the artist behind it." He leans forward. "Your cratepock won't change anything if you don't believe in it and embody it with your beliefs. People make change, not tools."

I frown. "That's all you think art is? A tool?"

"Not all of it," he says, "but if you're going on about changing the world, you need to know what you're doing. Or else you'll change it for the worse."

"You've never thought about changing the world?"

"Of course I have. Everyone has."

"What would you want to do?"

"That's not important."

"It's important to me." I blow a strand of hair out of my face. "Tell me."

Odin hesitates. He looks around his room like he wants to escape, to hide under his bed or inside his closet. Finally he says, "I want a world without bullies."

My gut squeals like I've been punched all over again. "That would be nice."

"I want a world where innocent people don't get hurt," he continues. "I want a world where kids aren't afraid to walk around at night in case they get attacked. That's . . . that's what I want. To not be—"

He cuts himself off abruptly, face twitching something fierce. It isn't until he inhales through his nose sharply that I realize what he's trying not to do.

"You should go home," he says, his voice thick. "My dad gets off work soon. He can drive you."

"Odin," I say, but I don't know what to say after that. I settle on, "It's okay—"

"What?" he barks. "You're telling me it's okay? You don't get anything about me. Don't act like you're some—some expert on anything. Okay?"

"I was going to say, it's okay to cry," I say quietly.

Odin scowls. "It's okay if you want to get beat up, sure. You can't show weakness. You can't—"

Something snaps in Odin, and he lunges toward me, and for a second I think he's going to tackle me, but instead he tears past me through the doorway and runs into the bathroom.

What is up with this guy?

While I wait for Odin to calm down—boy, I hope he calms down—I grab his sketchbook and flip to the most recent page, where my face looks out at me, showing all the strength and power Odin seems to think I possess.

I take a picture of it with my phone and set it to my background.

Shortly after that, Odin emerges from the bathroom, seemingly back in control. "I think my dad's home," he says.

"Okay," I say. "Thanks for having me over. This was really fun. We should do it again sometime."

Odin's tough face falls apart, but he doesn't cry. He looks relieved that he didn't scare me away. "Yeah," he says, and he almost smiles. Almost.

"Odin," a voice calls from downstairs. "Is someone here?"

"I brought someone over," he calls back. "You need to take him home."

Odin's dad comes upstairs. "Well, that's nice of you to let me know. Hi, I'm Mr. Thompson."

"Alan," I say. He looks like the guy in the framed photo downstairs.

"You didn't tell me you made a friend," Mr. Thompson says.

"We were doing art stuff," Odin says.

"Well, come on, Alan, let's get you home. Coming, O?"

"I'll stay here."

Odin and I stare at each other for a few awkward seconds. Do I shake his hand? He wouldn't want me to hug him, that's for sure. I settle on a half nod, a tip of the head, which he returns.

As I walk downstairs, I glance back at Odin, who's staring at me. Not an angry stare for once. This one's . . . sad? "See you," I call.

He waves.

"So, you know Odin from school?" Mr. Thompson asks me in the car.

"Yeah," I say. "We have ASPEN classes together."

Mr. Thompson smiles. "Well, it's great to see Odin make a friend."

A friend. Odin didn't exactly say we were friends—but he didn't deny it either.

Mr. Thompson puts on some talk radio, and we don't

say anything for most of the trip. After we've driven for a few minutes, I ask, "Mr. Thompson?"

"What is it, Alan?"

"Does Odin really have a chlorine allergy?"

Mr. Thompson doesn't say anything at first. "No," he eventually whispers. "He doesn't."

"Then he doesn't know how to swim?"

"He knows how to swim."

And that's it. That's as far as I want to pry. I don't want to butt in to Odin's past, whatever it may be. So I'm content to leave it at that.

Mr. Thompson, however, isn't. "I guess Odin told you the rest."

Odin didn't tell me anything.

"It's hard," Mr. Thompson murmurs. "He hasn't had a normal year. Things got . . . difficult at his old school. Very difficult."

My heart seizes up. I still keep quiet.

Mr. Thompson makes a turn, but I can tell he's not focused on the road. "We moved away from it all. I wanted to give him a fresh start. But he still has scars—not just mental ones."

Don't want to change in front of the gay kid, huh?

We drive in agonizing, miserable silence. What could have happened?

Mr. Thompson shakes his head. "I'm sorry to trail

off like this. Odin's had a hard time readjusting. I got so excited seeing him bring a friend home, it made me think things were getting better. Thanks for being so supportive."

Once Mr. Thompson drops me off, I walk inside 16 Werther Street and find Mom getting dinner ready. The full weight of the day, from fighting with Zack and Madison to getting beat up by Ron to picturing whatever horrible things happened to Odin for whatever reason, crushes me, and I run over to Mom and give her a massive, smothering hug. She gasps in surprise but returns the hug, and before I know it I'm sobbing over her shirt, my mind refusing to wrap itself around such a horrible, horrible thing.

I thought you of all people would understand. When you've been picked on your whole life for something, to get attention from someone you thought would never look at you for two seconds, that's incredible.

Just wait. Next time's going to be even worse.

I want a world where kids aren't afraid to walk around at night in case they get attacked. That's . . . that's what I want.

Odin . . . there's nothing I can do to make this better. This act of horror, this colossal burden he has to deal with, this is something he's got to handle for the rest of his life. What can I do?

What can I do but be his friend?

That's never going to be enough. But if, in some way, in some small, minuscule, barely significant way, I helped him, then maybe it'll be worth it. And maybe I can be worthy of all that strength and power Odin drew inside my eyes.

SIXTEEN

Thursday morning I decide to ride my bike to school instead of taking the bus. Well, I say "I decide"—really, Mom forces me into it by deciding she wants me to take my detention in the morning instead of the afternoon. When I ask her why, she looks at the floor and mutters, "There aren't as many kids at school in the morning." I never told her about round two with Ron, but my breakdown in her arms kind of hinted that something was up yesterday. She even says she wants to drive me to school herself so I don't run into anyone on the way. I say it's fine and tell her I'm riding my bike instead.

And you know what? I don't mind it. I don't mind her being overprotective. It means she still loves me.

It also means she didn't tell Dad about the detention. Guess she still knows how to keep a secret. And when she asked why I got the detention, and I said, "Just fooling around," she looked relieved, like I hadn't been in another fight. That she knows of.

So Mom's already on my good side, but when I leave for school, she says to me, "Your eye looks a lot better."

"Yeah," I say.

"Soon it'll be almost like it never happened."

I don't say anything.

She cups her hands around my chin. Her hands are warm and soft, like heated silk. "Promise me you'll be careful."

I want to protest like the rebellious, bratty tween I am, but I can't help looking into her eyes. The lines around them seem more stretched out today, the bags underneath sag a little lower. For the first time in my life, I think of my mother as old, even though I know she's not. And I can tell, for the first time in my life, she's thinking the same thing about me.

"I promise."

Evergreen is farther away from 16 Werther Street than Helen's Crest is, and the November morning air cuts right through my coat and jeans, filling my body with a crisp chill that makes me feel like I'm an apple being bit into by the wind. By the time I reach the school entrance, I'm cold, sweaty, and exhausted, which makes for an unpleasant combo, like mustard and mayonnaise.

As I walk to Miss Richter's room, I get a text from Odin:

So you're not going to the dance with that girl anymore

I write back:

nope. my dad hasn't mentioned it since I went to the mall with her.

Now you need a date

I skid to a halt so hard my shoes leave marks on the floor. He keeps going:

If you still want to go

To the dance

It's a week from tomorrow

The Winter Dance

At Evergreen

I write:

I'm probably not even going. I don't dance.

Did you buy a ticket

yeah.

Then you might as well go

I'm going

My dad is making me go

He says it could be a fun social activity

I don't want fun social activities

All I want to do is draw

haha yeah. I can relate. well if you're going maybe it won't be so bad.

We could go together

I almost drop my phone.

To the dance

The Winter Dance

It's a week from tomorrow

Is he—is Odin Thompson asking me to the dance?

is this a date?

What no

Why would it be a date

you said "we could go together." that sounds like a date to me.

It doesn't have to be

Forget it it's a stupid idea

it's not a stupid idea!

I grip my phone so tightly I expect it to crack. Thirty seconds go by. One minute. Two minutes. Nothing from Odin. You don't go silent after maybe sort of asking someone to the dance!

Was he even asking me to the dance at all? Does that make him—could it mean he's—

"Good morning," Miss Richter calls from her room. "You've been pacing back and forth outside for about five minutes."

"Uh, morning," I say, blushing. I'll see Odin soon enough, and then we can get this all sorted out. Assuming he even wants to talk to me again after I wasn't immediately receptive to his maybe-kind-of-possibly dance-asking-to.

"I hope you brought something to do," my teacher says as I take my desk in the square. "You're in trouble, so I'm not supposed to entertain you."

"I brought homework."

"That better not be my homework you waited until this morning to do."

I hold up the paper. "Math problems. They're not due until tomorrow."

Miss Richter nods, taking a big swig of coffee.

We work in silence, me plotting graphs and her doing whatever teacher-y stuff teachers do before class in the mornings. Until she says, "Actually, if you can put off doing your math homework, I could use your help with something."

"Is it as fun as cleaning your whiteboard?" That's what I did in the last detention I had with Miss Richter.

She shakes her head. "This one's even better. I was hoping to get your help with a lesson plan."

A lesson plan? Now I'm interested. "What is it?"

"Are you familiar with *The Art of War*?"

"Is it a painting?"

"It's a book. It originates from the fifth century BCE, supposedly by a renowned military strategist named Sun Tzu. We're coming into a unit on warfare and various wars and military leaders, so I thought it would be good for the students to have a grasp on some of the basics."

"I'm not really an expert on war, Miss Richter."

"That's okay." She opens a tiny black book and flips to a bookmarked page. "What do you think of when you hear this quote? 'The supreme art of war is to subdue the enemy without fighting.'"

"Uh, how do you win a war without fighting?"

"That's the question, isn't it? Sun Tzu had some ideas. What are yours?"

"Gee, uh, I guess . . . well, people always say you can win fights by being kind. I don't think that's true though."

"Why not?"

Just wait. Next time's going to be even worse. "I mean, there's a lot of mean people out there, and you can't exactly be nice to them and expect them to go away and leave you alone, right?"

Miss Richter considers this. "You don't have any experience with problem solving through kindness?"

I picture Nathan, defeated after CvC, willing to give up his dark, fiery ways because I stood up for him to

Dad. Mom, getting her voice and purpose back because I believed in her. Madison and Zack, standing by me because I helped them feel better about themselves.

"Okay," I say, "maybe a little."

Miss Richter takes another sip of coffee. "That's one way you can interpret the quote. But it's not quite what Sun Tzu had in mind. *The Art of War* talks about the importance of preparation. If you're truly prepared before a battle, he says, you'll have already won it before a single shot is fired."

"Yeah, but how do you do that? You can't always know everything about someone."

"I wonder," Miss Richter says. She sets the book down and closes it. "Sun Tzu believed that if you could force your opponent to accept your demands without fighting, you could maintain your resources and focus on other important goals in the future. So how could someone become truly prepared for a fight, force the other party to accept their demands, and maybe even problem solve through kindness?"

My head is swimming so much it feels like an aquarium. "I don't know, Miss Richter. I'm not a general. I'm a kid. Sorry I can't be more helpful."

I go back to doing math problems, but my heart isn't in them. If Miss Richter was trying to make me feel better, all she did was make me feel stupid.

"Did you see Talia's display when you came in?"

"Huh?" Then I remember: I gave her my photocretpoj yesterday. It must be up there now. Hanging. On display. Waiting for everyone to see it. To bare my soul.

You've got a good soul. You shouldn't mind showing it off.

"I liked it," my teacher says. "I hope you applied to the Gladstone Art Academy. Someone with your skill could benefit from a program like that."

Now she's gone from making me feel stupid to making me incredibly embarrassed. Someone with my skill? Someone whose greatest artistic contribution to the world had to be pried from his screaming, crying fingers? "Thanks," I murmur.

"Do you remember, after the business with your brother, when I asked you what was next for Alan Cole? Do you remember what you said?"

"I said, 'Can I get back to you?'"

"Yes. That's what you said. And I said that it's okay to not know, and what matters is that you keep looking. Do you remember that?"

I nod.

Miss Richter stands up. "Every student I've taught at Evergreen Middle School has left here a different person than they were when they arrived. Many for the better. Some, sadly, for the worse. Most students experience change gradually, over the course of many months. For some students, however, change is akin to getting an anvil dropped on their heads—it all squishes out at once, and often leaves a whopping headache in its wake."

She approaches my desk. "You, Alan, are at a crossroads. You've been hit by at least one anvil of change already, but there's another one looming overhead. This is the beginning. This is all just the beginning for you."

My sweaty/cold combo has come back with a vengeance. Miss Richter's never talked to me like this before.

"Someday soon," she continues, "you'll answer that question. What's next for Alan Cole? And then you'll know how to subdue the enemy without fighting." She pauses over my desk. "I believe in you. Even when you tackle other students. Don't forget that."

I don't know what to say. Is she serious? War? A crossroads? "Uh, th-thanks? Miss Richter, what do you mean by—"

But my teacher is already back at her desk. "I can't tell you. You've got to figure it out for yourself. I'm here if you want to talk in a safe space, but I can't—I won't—tell you the answers." She smiles. "Ah, to be twelve again."

"But—"

"Thanks for the help," she says. "I think this is going to be a strong lesson."

I glumly return to my math homework, head spinning with new concepts and information. I'd rather feel stupid or embarrassed than overwhelmed.

In the middle of it all though, my favorite teacher said she believes in me. Even when I screw up. I've never had an adult tell me they believed in me before. Knowing that, and remembering all the people around me I've problem solved for through kindness, might help me navigate this crossroads—even if the anvil of change gives me a colossal headache.

After my early morning detention, once the rest of the school arrives, I make my way to the "Where Do We Come From?" display. The number of "stories" is up to seven. It looks like Meredith Wood added in a pipe cleaner doll meant to be herself, but that's not why I'm here—I'm here to look at my cretpoj, on display next to Odin's dragon picture. The tag underneath reads:

ALAN COLE
Sapling

No title. No fanfare. Just my name and grade.

I brace myself for all kinds of questions and comments and feedback—what if someone thinks I've painted too much shading around the eyes, or the strokes of my cheekbones were too broad—but nobody comes up to me. There's not even anybody around the display, really. Just me and—

"Wow," Zack says, skipping up to me like we didn't have a friendship-ending fight yesterday. "Is that it? Your cretpoj?"

I nod.

He tilts his head to the side. "It really looks like you."

"Thanks."

Zack attempts to reorient his head but he goes off-balance and bumps into a passing kid. "I think it's great you decided to show it off. What changed your mind?"

I almost say Odin, but I don't. "I got some advice."

"Cool." Zack smiles. "I'm proud of you. Oh, hi, Madison!" Zack chirps as Madison walks by.

Madison ignores Zack. He steps up to the "Where Do We Come From?" wall. "Hmm," he says. "It looks just like you."

"Thanks."

He's still ticked about yesterday, and probably for good reason. Zack is going off about this dance he's invented—"you shimmy your left hip, then you shimmy your right hip, then you wiggle your toes, then you shimmy your earlobe"—and Madison's barely paying attention, and I really want to say something, but I have no idea what to say, and this continues on for a little bit until Madison finally says, "I'm proud of you."

"Really?"

He nods. "You did well."

"Thanks," I say. "That . . . means a lot." They're both proud of me, even after we kicked up dirt all over our friendship yesterday.

Behind us, Zack is still babbling about the Zack Shuffle—"there's a lot of butt wagging in this part, I hope Principal Dorset doesn't put his foot down and say we can't do it, but I think as long as he sees how fun it is he'll come around—"

"Zack," I say, "let's have a sleepover this weekend."

Zack stops talking. "Okay!" he cheers.

"A sleepover?" Madison asks, looking around nervously. "I'll have to check with Meredith."

"Yeah, and I'll need to check with Heppy," Zack says. "We're taking a gondola to New Jersey this weekend."

"Guys," I say, "let's make hanging out with each other a priority. No Meredith, no June, no whatever her name is."

"Countess Hepzibah Mergatroid III. She goes to the Catholic school up the street."

I smile. "Let's have some friend time. Sound good?"

"Sounds good to me!" Zack yells.

Madison slowly smiles. "Sure. I'll tell Meredith I've got a prior engagement."

As we enter homeroom, I realize I'm okay being Madison's prior engagement. So long as I'm on his schedule.

"Looks like you can rest easy, Galan," someone says as they walk by.

Huh? What does she—

A loud clanging noise erupts from the bathroom, and Ron storms out, soaking wet. A few people laugh as he stomps by, leaving wet footprints. Connor emerges from the bathroom, smirking. "Sorry, guess that sink's a little strong," he calls.

Ron doesn't even seem to notice me as he walks past. He keeps his face down and his shoulders slumped. Never run from a fight indeed. It feels good to see him suffer, to watch him get knocked around for a change.

Back in homeroom, Odin's at his desk. He doesn't look up when I sit down. I clear my throat. "Hi."

"Hey."

The carefully constructed question I was going to ask evaporates. Instead I take my seat, waiting for words to materialize. I settle on, "So—"

"Not here," Odin whispers.

"So that *was* a—"

"I said not here. Text me later."

"Okay."

Zack is bugging Julie Linder about something to do with squirrels (as usual) and Madison and Talia are arguing about whether James Madison should be on Mount Rushmore (also as usual), and I, very quietly, say, "You know, it could be kind of nice."

Odin flips a page in his book.

That's all I say. For now.

"Hey, Alan," Connor says. "Did you see Ron today? It looked like he peed his pants."

"Yeah, that was pretty great," I say. I smile at the memory of Ron, totally humiliated, power walking down the hall away from laughter. I smile even more at the thought of Connor maybe punching Ron in the gut or giving Ron a black eye or calling Ron garbage or—

Or . . .

. . . Oh no.

I know that smile on my face.

It's Nathan's, when Nathan dedicated his life to ruining mine.

It's Dad's.

It's not mine.

But there it is. On my face.

"Man, he really had it coming," Connor says. "He's such a loser."

"Yeah," I whisper. "He's a loser."

Connor takes out his spearmint-scented gum and makes kissy lips at Sheila.

Why am I not reveling in Ron's destruction? Ron, who's made me into target practice, who threatened to beat up my friends, who stands in opposition to all of my values, who thinks I'm literal garbage? Am I trying to problem solve through kindness when I should be waging war?

SEVENTEEN

After English, Odin—who's been silent all day, both verbally and via text—says to me, "I want to come over to your house."

I choke on my own tongue. "Today?"

"Yeah. You came over yesterday. We could take turns."

He wants to hang out. A lot. Wow.

But even Zack and Madison have never hung out at 16 Werther Street. The environment there is toxic to humans. Visitors have been known to develop extra limbs or eye sockets. "My family's kind of—not great with people."

"It'll be fine," Odin says, and before I know it he's following me onto bus 19. We sit next to each other, and I try to ignore the sensation in my gut of bungee jumping without a net.

A chime goes off in my pocket: my phone.

It's not a date

Odin's phone is out, his thumbs rapidly poking the screen. I get another text:

But if it was would that be a problem

My face heats up. I write back:

I guess not.

I immediately curse under my breath. "I guess"? Did that come off as sarcastic or cold?

If it was a date would you wear a tuxedo

I snort.

yeah. white and purple.

I would wear a cape

And a top hat

would you do magic tricks?

I would pull a bunny out of my hat

The bunny would also be wearing a cape and top hat

I chuckle.

haha.

If it was a date would we hold hands

My face heats to volcanic levels.

we could.

I want to look at Odin to see what his always-stoic

face has turned into. Is he blushing? Smiling? Grimacing? But I'm too scared to turn my neck.

If it was a date would we

would we what?

"Odin Thompson," Talia says from the seat in front of us, "you don't normally go on this bus."

Odin's phone is already away. "I like to mix it up."

"I see. Alan Cole, why is your face so red?"

That only makes it redder. "I, uh, guess I'm feeling kind of hot."

"Are you aware that it's currently twenty-seven degrees outside?"

"Fahrenheit or Celsius?"

"Funny. I'd recommend wearing short sleeves tomorrow if this keeps up. You don't want to walk around looking like a tomato with a bruise over its eye."

She turns back around, but Odin doesn't take out his phone again for the rest of the ride.

"If it was a date would we" what?

The grand tour of the house ends with my room. "That's Big Green," I say, gesturing to the sugar maple outside my window. "It's more like Big Red and Yellow during fall, and Big Lot of Nothing for the winter, but I didn't want to keep changing the name. I like to paint Big Green. Want to see some pictures?"

"Yeah."

I show Odin pictures from my old sketchbook, some of which nobody else has ever seen. "Don't look at the ones in the front, those are really rough," I say. "I get better as it goes along."

Odin is immersed in my sketchbook. It's fun to watch him flip through the pages, his hand flexing slightly with each turn. One time he actually runs his fingers along the paper, over a particularly lifelike sketch of the dishes in the sink.

"If it was a date would we" what?

Sing campfire songs? Paint our faces purple? *Dance?* (Even though I don't dance?)

This is stupid. He's right in front of me. We don't have to worry about being overheard. We can talk like sensible people. Right? "Hey, Odin?"

He looks up.

My door opens.

"You seen the glue?" Nathan asks, walking into my room. "Me and Marcellus are making—" He notices Odin in the corner.

"No, I don't have the glue," I say. I look behind Nathan and say, "Hi, Marcellus."

Marcellus nods, standing in the shadow of the doorframe.

"Where's what's-their-faces?" Nathan asks. "Buzz

Cut and Bird's Nest?"

"They're not here," I say.

"I didn't think you were friends with . . . what's your name again? Odor? Ogre?"

"Yeah, I'm Ogre," Odin says. "And you're a troll."

Nathan crosses his arms.

"Come on," Marcellus says. "Let's give them some privacy."

"Privacy? Why would—" Nathan's eyes dart from me to Odin, and he grins. "Right. Privacy. Got it." He shuts the door.

I bury my face in my hands. "Sorry. He's a little hard to handle sometimes. It's tough to believe, but he's gotten a *lot* better."

"He doesn't seem as bad as Ron at least," Odin says. "At least that Connor guy is doing his job."

"Yeah . . ."

"What?"

"I don't know. I just . . ."

Odin shakes his head at me. "You know what your problem is?"

"Aside from my awful sketching and my nightmare of a brother and the fact that my name can be combined into many different food products?"

"You're too nice."

"Too nice?"

"You don't like it that Ron's getting picked on."

I sigh. "You said it yourself: nobody deserves to be bullied."

Odin's voice is hard as flint. "Homophobes don't count."

"I know, I know, but—but I hate to see anyone get hurt. Even Ron."

The room falls into silence. If Odin had a bad experience at his old school with bullies, it makes sense that he'd be so adamant about how they "don't count." He might see me as a "bully sympathizer." He might not even want to be my friend anymore.

"You know what my problem is?" he asks.

I brace myself for "you."

"My problem is your problem doesn't bother me."

"Huh?"

"Actually . . . I like it. I like that you're so nice." He looks out the window at Big Green, swaying in the breeze.

My heart swells up like a hot air balloon. "Thanks."

He rummages around his bag for his own sketchbook. "Come on. Let's make art."

"If it was a date would we" what?

I don't know. With Nathan in potential earshot of any conversation, I might never know.

* * *

"Pretty good," Odin says at the end of our art marathon, flexing his wrist. "You're improving. Your shading is a lot more detailed."

"Thanks," I say, stretching in my chair.

"It's a shame I'll be getting into Gladstone and not you."

"You wish."

"More like I know. I'm definitely the better artist."

"So you say."

"So I know. I'm getting in, and you're not."

"Victoria Gladstone isn't going to care about anime people."

He doesn't reply. Did I go too far? He's the one who started it! "Where's your bathroom?" he asks, standing up.

"Down the hall."

At least he's not running in there to cry. I hope.

Odin's left my door open, and Mom pokes her head in. "Do you have a friend over?"

"Yeah. Can you drive him home? I think we're wrapping things up."

"Or he could stay for dinner."

Oh God. If I wanted to scare Odin away, sure. Nathan was bad enough, but Dad? "I think he's got to get going—"

"Who's got to get going?" Odin asks, reappearing at the door.

Mom introduces herself and extends the offer to feast at the dinner table of shadow and darkness. I shake my head behind her and make a throat-cutting motion with my hands, but whether Odin doesn't see me or he's getting me back for insulting his anime art style, he says, "Sure."

And right on cue, the front door slams shut.

This can only end in tragedy.

"This isn't good," I say as we make our way downstairs.

"You can stay for dinner tomorrow," Odin says.

He's already planning tomorrow. Whoa. "That's not—"

We arrive at the table and Dad is already there, waiting for his wife to serve him. His eyes take in the two of us. "Dad," I say, "this is, uh, my friend Odin."

Odin tips his head in a nod.

Dad eyes Odin up. "I didn't think you had any friends."

"You've met Madison."

"Of course. How could I forget such a winning personality." He takes a sip of water.

Odin gives me a look. I mouth, "Told you."

Mom's brought a fifth chair and some extra place settings in, so Odin sits next to me. Nathan walks into the kitchen and stops. "He's staying for dinner?"

"Where's Marcellus?" Odin asks.

My brother grumbles, "He knows better than to stay for dinner."

Odin at least had the good fortune to come on a night where Mom cooked and didn't order fast food; tonight is pasta with meat sauce. "You're not a vegetarian, are you, Odin?" she asks.

"I'm not," Odin says.

"Vegetarian," Dad mutters. "If you were vegetarian, I'd have kicked you out."

I can't tell if that's a joke or not. Odin's face is, as usual, blank.

We eat in silence for a little while, the ticking of the old wooden clock and the scraping of silverware on plates the only sounds. Eventually Mom asks, "So, Odin, do you have class with Alan?"

"Yeah, we have ASPEN together."

"You're not the guy who gave him that shiner, are you?" Dad asks.

"No way. I'd never hurt Alan."

The way he says that makes my body feel like feathers floating high above the clouds.

"Except I'm getting into Gladstone, and he's not."

Now the feathers turn into fifty-pound weights and crash to the earth.

"Gladstone?" Dad asks.

I choke on a stray bit of penne. Yeah, Odin probably overheard me tell Madison and Zack that Dad didn't want me to go to Gladstone anymore, but I haven't mentioned it to him directly since. He probably thinks it's blown over by now. Just my luck.

"It's a big art academy in Philly," Odin continues, oblivious. "They only take one kid per school."

Dad barks out a laugh. "That thing? Alan's not going to that. I'm enrolling him in boxing lessons instead."

Mom shifts in her seat. Looks like she hasn't told Dad about my application yet.

"You're an artist too then, huh?" Dad asks.

"Yeah," Odin replies.

"Do you get a lot of girls?"

Odin stops scooping his pasta. I want to bury my face in wet cement.

"I didn't think so," Dad grumbles. "You probably don't even have a date for the Winter Dance."

"Jimmy," Mom says quietly, "about the art academy—"

"I found out yesterday Alan isn't going with June anymore," Dad continues. "Mr. Harrison says June changed her mind. She insisted it was all her and not him."

Whew. At least June followed through.

"Of course," Dad continues, "this puts my promotion at risk. This whole family could fall overboard at any given moment. But Alan doesn't care about that. Why would he? He's an 'artist.' They don't have any concept of reality. If you ask me, June wanted to be with a real man. Someone who doesn't waste his time drawing. Someone who knows how to fight back when he gets punched in the face."

My black eye throbs.

"Do you see what I mean?" Dad asks Odin. "I'm sure your parents don't want you doing art. They want you to be a good, obedient child who knows reality from a hole in the ground." He takes a sip of water.

"No offense," Odin says, "but you don't have a clue what anyone at this table wants."

My throat turns inside out.

Dad sets his glass gently down. "Excuse me?"

I kick Odin's leg under the table. He ignores me. "Art is amazing," he says. "Sketching and painting make me feel great. Artists can change the world, definitely more than whatever you do for a living."

Mom runs her fingers along the cross around her neck. Nathan's eyes ping back and forth between everyone at the table.

"And as far as dating goes," Odin keeps going, "we're in seventh grade. We've got plenty of time. It's not—"

"Enough."

Odin stops talking.

Gulp. Gulp. Gulp. Dad's water disappears down his throat. He places the glass on the table, his eyes never leaving Odin's. "I can see why Alan is friends with you."

"Dad," I say. "Stop."

Something about the tone of my voice shakes something up in Dad's brain. He stares at his hands for a few seconds, then says, "Kids these days. Can't laugh at a joke."

Odin looks at me.

Dad stands up. "Thank you for coming over," he says, and heads for the garage.

Mom clears the plates. "I hope you liked the food, Odin."

"It was good, thanks," he says. "Better than my dad's cooking."

I bet Odin's dad doesn't call him a loser in front of company though. That seems like a pretty safe bet.

That night, as I grind out my homework, I get a text:

Your dad's nice

I warned you.

He listened to you though

When you said stop

He stopped

I know. that was weird, that never happens. maybe I reminded him that he's supposed to be improving.

You stood up for me

To him

I guess? it didn't feel like standing up.

It was

hey Odin?

Hey

if it was a date would we what?

He's silent for a few minutes. But right when I give up and put the phone to the side of my desk:

Would we

Keep it secret

The screen of my phone glows in the dim light of my room.

only if you want to.

I don't hear from him for the rest of the night, though I check my phone every two minutes to make sure he hasn't texted me and I somehow missed it.

Being Madison and Zack's friend was never this complicated.

EIGHTEEN

Friday morning I walk by the "Where Do We Come From?" display to briefly admire my photocretpoj, shining brightly among the other self-portraits. It's been twenty-four hours. No comments. No gasps of recognition. No sudden, world-changing bolts of inspiration. I guess that's okay though. I mean, it has only been twenty-four hours. If there's still no response after the weekend, then I can start crying foul.

When Zack ambles into homeroom, he walks by my desk. "Hi, Alan. I came up with this card game for the sleepover. It's like blackjack, but threes cut your score in half, and when you're dealt a five you have to sing a Janet Jackson song. And my mom let me rent a scary movie! There's going to be so much to do. We won't be getting any sleep at all."

From across the room, Madison says, "Yes, it's going to be fun. But, if you want my honest opinion, you need to promise to be a little less—" He tries to find the right word.

"Skullpocritical?" Zack asks.

Madison shakes his head. "No, I—skullpowhat?"

"You know," Zack says, "when your skull does something hypocritical. Like rolling your brain around when it should be paying attention."

Madison sighs. "Just calm down."

It's nice to see my friends acting like their old selves again. But . . . Odin isn't in the desk next to me for some reason. This worries me, but maybe he got his shoelace stuck in his locker, or he's spending a really long time combing his hair in the bathroom. It's probably fine.

During the morning announcements, when I have to listen to Principal Dorset drone on about the Winter Dance decorations committee and the Winter Dance fundraising committee and the Winter Dance Elvis impersonator committee (I might have made up one of those), some of the other kids in homeroom are looking at their phones and giggling and then looking at *me*. Oh boy. It's probably a funny text about how maybe I have oatmeal stuck in my teeth or my fly is down. (Check: the Tupperware is vacuum sealed.) Nothing to worry about.

Walking down the hall though . . . I get plenty of stares. It's like I'm back to being the face of bullying at Evergreen again—people keep staring, and a lot of people keep laughing. What gives?

Zack walks me to swimming, like he used to. "You and Odin have been hanging out a lot, huh?"

"Sort of," I say. "He came over yesterday."

Zack's face looks like there's a loose screw poking him in the foot when he walks. "Yeah. I bet that was pretty cool." I notice him grab something small and rock-shaped in his pocket—his special rock, the gift bestowed upon him by his late father. That's when I know Zack is really lost in thought.

"You okay?" I ask.

"Huh? Oh yeah—just thinking about stuff. No big deal." He smiles and leaves me at the locker room.

Loud laughter echoes off the tinny walls as I change. I still don't see Odin. "Hey Galan," someone asks, "where's your boyfriend?"

Huh? "My what?"

"You know," another guy says. "The guy you're in love with. Everyone's talking about it."

Uh-oh. "What . . . do you mean?"

Jamal Lawrence takes out his phone and shows me: "There's a text going around the school about how you and Odin were making out in the cafeteria the other day."

"Uh . . . that never happened—"

More guys come over and laugh at me. I still don't see Odin anywhere. And someone else is missing too. Where's Ron?

"That's enough," Marcellus says to the crowd. "Get in the pool area."

"Yeah, we want to give Alan and Odin their privacy," someone says, making kissy lips at me.

I'm deathly pale and shaking. "This doesn't make sense," I say to Marcellus. "If it happened in the cafeteria, everyone would have seen it, right? But it didn't happen. Why does everyone believe it?"

"People believe what they want to believe," Marcellus says.

I take a deep breath. "Where's Odin?"

"I don't know."

"Okay. Where's—"

And in walks Ron, late for class. He bolts onto the bench but freezes in place when he sees me.

"You," I say. "You did this."

There's no look of triumph on Ron's face, no grinning laughter. He looks as unhappy as a clown at a funeral, as usual. "I don't know what you're talking about."

Marcellus hovers by my side, on hand to prevent a potential round three.

"This text that's floating around," I say. "You spread it."

"You can't prove anything."

"Where's Odin?"

"Your boyfriend? I don't know where he is."

"He's not my boyfriend!"

"Could've fooled me. The way you two look at each other all the time is sick. Plus the making out in the cafeteria."

"There was no making out in the cafeteria!"

"You want to go, Galan? I'll kick your butt again if you try to mess with me, suspension or no suspension. Too bad your boyfriend's not here to pick you up off the dirt, huh?"

Marcellus steps between us. "Get in the bleachers—"

"You crossed the line," I say. "You really—"

Ron, for the briefest of seconds, blinks, looks away, retreats inward.

And it hits me. Looking into Ron's eyes, seeing his macho posturing and his desire to act like the toughest guy in the room, and thinking of that outburst about his dad, I'm reminded of BC (Before Cretpoj) Era me, the me who analyzed anyone's face I could to learn about them and maybe capture them inside a work of art. And I wonder . . . maybe I'm not the only face that deserves to be captured inside a cretpoj.

So I shrug and walk past Ron on the way to the pool, and I dive into the water for a brief period of time. This is expressly forbidden and could get me into a heap of trouble (and it *does*, because Coach Streit blows her whistle and makes me sit on the bleachers for half the class). But I had to do it. I've swum a lot over the past few weeks, but this was one of the first times the water felt good. Necessary. Cleansing.

For the ten seconds I was in the pool, I was in control. And nobody could take that away from me.

The day is long, but I get through it. Connor says, no fewer than three times, he's going to "make Ron pay." I've never seen him this mad. I've never really seen him mad at all, come to think of it. At the end of English class, he grumbles that he's going to "wait until the perfect opportunity to get Ron back." That makes me a little afraid for Ron, which is an idea I never thought I'd come close to thinking.

I still don't know what happened to Odin. I tried texting him tons of times but he didn't respond to any of them. I can handle the laughter and the staring. But I can't handle my friends being hurt.

Before I know it, it's another dinner at 16 Werther Street. I pour salt on my french fries and try to imagine myself anywhere else. Eating pizza at Zack's apartment, drinking a smoothie with Madison at Helen's Crest, using a water fountain alongside Odin (God, I hope Odin's okay)—anything will do. But instead I'm stuck here, in this house, with this family, from now until the end of time.

Like a karate chop through the cinder block of dinner, Nathan says, "So there's this workshop offered at the community college. Can I go?"

"What kind of workshop?" Mom asks.

"Engineering," Nathan says. I had no idea he was interested in engineering.

"How much?" Dad asks.

"A couple hundred bucks."

Mom says, "That sounds great. It's so nice to see you interested in someth—"

"We can't afford it," Dad cuts her off. "If I told Alan no, I'm telling you no too."

"Jimmy," Mom says quietly, "I mailed Alan's application already."

Dad's eyes turn to thunder, but Mom sits up tall, doesn't bow under the storm. "We can make it work," she says. "Our kids want to follow their dreams."

"Dreams?" he barks. "Life isn't about dreams. Dreams just get in the way. Next time you pay a massive amount of money for some silly dream, consult me first. Especially since I'm not getting my promotion anymore because one member of this family put himself first."

"We didn't pay anything yet," Mom says. "He has to get in first. But he will."

That makes warmth sprout inside me like a seed, countering the slick poison seeping down my insides from Dad.

But Dad isn't listening. "And Nathan, since when have you cared about engineering?" he asks.

Nathan squeezes a fry in his fist. "Since always."

"Bah." Dad waves a hand. "We don't have time for dreams."

The table goes quiet again for a little bit.

"God," Nathan says, "it's like you don't care at all."

The heat in the dining room is all-consuming. Dad slowly sets his water down. "What did you say?"

"I thought you were trying to be a better person. What happened to that?"

Dad glares at Nathan. "This isn't my fault. Even if I wanted to send you to this workshop, we can't afford that and Alan's art thing. If you want to blame someone, blame your brother."

"No," he says. "I'm done blaming my brother."

The full impact of the words slams into me all at once. He'd always blamed me for everything wrong in our family when I didn't even do anything wrong, and now, to hear him say this, in front of everyone—

"I'm so sick of this crap," Nathan says. "It's always the same. You never put us first. You never put anyone other than *you* first. I'm sick of it! I'm—"

"That's enough," Dad says, cutting through Nathan's speech like a knife through plastic.

Except not today. Today, Nathan's not plastic. He's cardboard. And it's not as easy to cut through cardboard with a knife. "It's always something," he continues. "Always some excuse why you can't be a good dad. I'm tired of excuses. I'm tired of *you* getting in my way."

Dad stands up. This manages to stop Nathan. But he still glares angrily at Dad.

"Jimmy," Mom cautions.

"So this is how it is," Dad says. "Do you believe this, Alan? Can you believe your brother is acting like this? After I work my tail off every day to put food on the table? To pay for everything he owns? I don't work every single day to pay for dreams that won't go anywhere. I work so my kids can get a good education and go on to careers where they can be successful, not to waste time on dreams. I had dreams once. I learned my lesson."

"Dad," I start.

"If you want to go to this workshop thing," Dad continues to Nathan, "pay for it yourself. You won't get a cent more from me."

Nathan rises to his feet, meeting Dad's eyes. Nathan's about the same height as Dad, but there's no doubt in the mind of anyone at this table that Dad's the bigger person in every other way. After a glare-off between the Coles, Nathan stomps upstairs.

Now it's Mom's turn to stand up. She runs after Nathan, leaving me and Dad at the dinner table.

Dad sits back down and resumes eating, but I've lost my appetite. "Dad."

His fork and knife stop moving.

I whisper, "Today . . . do your best."

I stand up and leave the table. For the first time, Dad's the last Cole at the dinner table.

As I walk upstairs, Mom is leaving Nathan's room, her face set in a rigid pattern. She and I make eye contact briefly, and for that small moment we're on the same page. I knock on Nathan's door.

"What?"

I crack open the door. "Hey."

Nathan's sitting at his desk, playing with one of his

little toys he made from elementary school. "What do you want?"

"Just checking to see if you're all right."

"I'm fine," he grumbles.

I shut the door behind me. "Engineering, huh?"

"That's right."

"I had no idea."

"There's a lot about me you don't know," Nathan says. "That nobody knows. I guess . . . I guess I freed up parts of my brain that were taken up with hating you."

I nod. It's one of the first times I've ever heard Nathan talk about our history so directly.

"I'm trying to move on," my brother says. "And Dad's not."

"I might not even get into the Gladstone Academy. So, uh, there's still a chance—"

"Oh, shut up. Quit being the nice one, will you? It's disgusting." He gives me a weak smile. "Nah, if I have to, I'll get some crappy job somewhere. There's got to be somebody out there hiring fourteen-year-olds."

"Okay," I say. I don't have anything to say after that. I hover around the doorway while Nathan spins his little top. "Well, you, uh, know where to find me if you want to talk?" I don't mean to end it on a question mark, but I do anyway.

"Yeah," Nathan says without looking up.

I turn around to open the door, but the door's already open, and Dad's standing in the doorway, looking not quite himself.

Nathan scowls. "What?"

Dad doesn't say anything. His eyes take in me and Nathan. Me, Nathan. Me, Nathan.

"What?" Nathan repeats. "I get it—you don't want me to go. That's fine. I'll pay for it myself. I'll cut lawns, or shovel snow, or deliver papers, or whatever other crappy job I need to get—"

"You can go."

"Huh?"

"I said you can go. You should still get a job to earn extra money, but you can go."

I can't believe what I'm hearing. This has to be some cosmic mistake. Our dad has been replaced with an alien, and as soon as he lulls us into false security he's going to suck out our brains through our nostrils.

Nathan says, very quietly, "You're serious?"

Dad takes a step into Nathan's room, making me take a few paces back. He breathes deep, once, twice, three times. He opens his eyes and says to Nathan, "Today, do your best." Then he leaves.

Nathan slowly reclines in his chair, exhaling. "Wow. I guess what I said really got to him. Awesome." He grins.

I walk back downstairs to help Mom with the dishes.

As I dry our plates, she gives me a kiss on the cheek, and it doesn't feel like she's trying too hard. Like it comes a little more naturally to her this time. Like maybe being somewhere else is overrated. Like maybe it's okay, for tonight at least, to be right here.

NINETEEN

"Slumber! Party! Slumber! Party! Slumber—"

"Hey, calm down," Ms. Kimble says.

"Yeah, you're going to burn yourself out," the man on the couch says.

"He won't," me, Madison, and Ms. Kimble all say at the same time.

At the Saturday up-all-night hang-out-a-thon, Ms. Kimble introduces me and Madison to Theo, her boyfriend, who's tall and thin and has plenty of lines around his eyes that say to the world he's filled up his frequent smiler card. Until Theo leaves the apartment, Zack's eyes are unfocused, and he acts even louder than normal, stomping around and making up chants and crossing the line from Tolerable to Obnoxious.

As we devour the rest of the pizza, Ms. Kimble goes

to bed, and we lower our volume to whispers (which in Zack's case is the volume of regular speech). "You guys want any of this garlic dipping sauce?" Zack asks. "It's really good."

Madison, having finished his pizza portion, has moved on to munching on "special popcorn" (which winds up being normal microwavable popcorn). He shakes his head at Zack.

"This is nice," I say, dipping my pizza crust in the sauce. "I'm glad we're doing this."

"Yeah," Zack says. "It'd be even better if my mom's boyfriend didn't come over."

"Theo?" Madison asks. "He seemed nice enough."

"Yeah, *Theo*," Zack says with more venom than I've ever heard him use.

I wipe my mouth with a napkin. "What's wrong with him? You've been acting strange about him ever since they started dating."

"I don't want to talk about it," Zack says.

"But you brought him up," Madison says.

"Fine." Zack lowers his voice like he's in a confessional. "I wish my mom stayed single, that's all."

"She seems happy with Theo though," Madison says.

Zack bites his lip.

And suddenly, I get it. "He won't replace him," I whisper.

"He's starting to," Zack murmurs. "His stuff keeps showing up around here. It's like he's . . . moving in."

"That doesn't mean she'll forget about your dad," I say. "Or that you will."

Zack's eyes drop to the table. "There's only three people in my life," he says. "And they're all in this apartment right now."

Madison and I look at each other.

Zack continues, "I don't want to l-lose any of you t-too." He lets out a huge sob. "D-Do you think I'm a b-bad p-p-person for not wanting my m-mom to b-be happy? Or you g-guys?"

I rub Zack's back. "You're the farthest thing from a bad person I know."

Zack sniffles.

"I'm sorry, Zack," Madison whispers. "I know I've been rude to you. Both of you."

"No," Zack gasps. "If you want t-to hang out with M-M-Meredith, you c-can. I won't stop you. I want you to b-be happy."

"But I'm not happy," Madison grumbles. "Not with her."

"Huh?" I ask, handing Zack a napkin. "I thought you liked her."

Madison puffs out his cheeks. "I did. Maybe. I don't

know. She's not a bad person. But I don't think . . . she's my type. Even though I'd love nothing more than for her to be." He sighs. "She doesn't care for either of you, you know."

Zack hiccups loudly.

"She tried to get me to stop hanging out with you. She told me you were both holding me back, that I could be one of the cool kids. All I had to do was keep the company of other cool kids."

"But you never sat with them at lunch," I say.

Madison shakes his head. "I couldn't. That table is our place in the cafeteria. It's our home. I couldn't break that. Even though I broke other things."

"It's okay," I say. "I said bad stuff too. I'm sorry."

"Now I don't know what to do," Madison continues. He runs a hand over his hair. "My parents found out about her. After they realized I wasn't making her up, they were *overjoyed*. They want to meet Meredith and Meredith's parents and Meredith's grandparents and Meredith's cousins and Meredith's pets, and they want me to exercise twice as much at Helen's Crest." He looks at Zack. "So no, that idea would have backfired tremendously."

Another hiccup.

"But I don't like her." Madison sighs. "I've gone my

whole life without any girls interested in me, and when I finally get one who is, I don't like her! Honestly, what a problem to have."

"You could go to the dance as friends," I say.

"That won't work. My parents are convinced this is my one shot to find a girlfriend. I'm twelve. That's a lot of pressure." He runs another hand over his hair. Then another.

"This dance is turning into a nightmare," I say.

Madison shifts his eyes around. "I want to like Meredith and her friends. I really do. It's been so hard to find people in my life who can look at me as something other than Fatison Truman, the fat boy. Of course, now I see there were two people all along who never looked at me like that."

I smile. "You okay?" I ask Zack, whose hiccups have subsided.

He nods. He blows his nose with the napkin, then wipes his eyes with the same napkin. "Wow, that felt good," he gasps. "Your turn," he says to me.

"Huh?" I ask.

"We both confessed something, now it's your turn," Zack says.

I blink. "I don't have anything to confess."

Zack and Madison look at each other.

"What?" I ask.

Zack blows his nose one more time. "It rhymes with 'snowed in.'"

What's he talking about? What kind of confession would I—

I turn bright red. "What, uh, about him?"

"Alan," Madison asks, "do you like Odin Thompson?"

Sweat starts prickling my back. "If this is because of that fake text about us kissing—"

"It's not."

"Then of course I don't like him. W-What gives you that idea?"

"The way you look at him," Zack says. "It's how you used to look at Connor. I pointed it out to Madison one day."

"That's silly," I say, waving a hand. "I look at lots of people, every day. I like to study faces. That doesn't mean I have crushes on all of them." Of course, I don't make portraits of everyone's faces either . . .

"It's okay," Zack says, standing up and throwing out his snotty napkins. "You can't help who you get crushes on. Right, Madison?"

"Right," Madison grumbles. "There's no point in 'trying out girls' if all you like is guys. You can't help that. I see that now."

"But I don't like him," I insist.

Zack and Madison look at each other. Again.

"Stop that," I say.

"Why don't you go to the dance with Odin?" Zack asks. "You don't have to go with June anymore. You can go with whoever you want."

"I . . . I don't know. If I liked Odin—which I don't—I'd have to explain it to my parents. And I don't even know if Odin is gay or not." I mean yeah, we've talked about going to the dance and holding hands, but Connor's always been friendly too, and he's as straight as a picket fence. I don't want to get my hopes up and fall for someone who can't reciprocate. Again. I glance at my phone, resting next to the pizza box. It's been all of yesterday and today. Nothing.

"That's fine," Zack says. "I'm going to be a good friend and support you no matter what."

There's so much swirling through my brain—getting my friends back and what to do about Odin and that glimpse, that microscopic glimpse, into Ron's soul. "I've got an idea," I say. "It's a little weird."

"We like weird," Zack says.

"Yes, weird is good," Madison says.

So how could someone become truly prepared for a fight, force the other party to accept their demands, and maybe even problem solve through kindness?

I smile. This is something I'm proud to talk about. "Let me tell you about my enthigacs."

TWENTY

It's a dreary, damp, chilly Sunday when I arrive at the Thompson residence. The up-all-night hang-out-a-thon was a success, even though we didn't quite stay up *all* night—by the count on Madison's watch, it was around 3:30 in the morning. I got a little sleep when I got home, enough to stay awake for this.

The enthigacs.

I'm taking a risk here. I don't know if Odin is even home, and if he is, I don't know if he's up for company. But it's a risk I'm willing to take. Mom is staying out front until I'm secured inside the house. "Have fun," she says.

I nod.

When I reach the door, Mom calls me back. "I'm proud of you," she says. "Making friends."

"Uh, thanks."

"I mean it. You've had a rough time. It takes a lot to come out of everything still smiling, but you do. I just wanted you to know that." She cups my chin in her hands, then runs a light finger over my left eye. It barely hurts.

Mr. Thompson, smiling broadly, lets me in. "Odin!" he calls. "You've got company."

Odin appears at the foot of the stairs, and I'm filled with such relief it practically seeps from my body onto the rug. Also, my cheeks flush immediately. Uh-oh. It's not that I like him. I'm embarrassed to be coming into his home on a Sunday afternoon. For some reason. Yeah, that must be it.

"What are you doing here?" he asks.

"You weren't returning my texts." I follow him inside his room; he shuts the door and I sit on his bed.

He sits at his desk, dark eyes glaring into space. "I got freaked out."

"Because of the rumor?"

"I called my dad to take me home on Friday once I heard the rumors. I can't go through that again. I *can't*."

Again?

"I have an idea," I say. "It's a way we can stand up for ourselves and take a stand against all the bullies at Evergreen."

"I can't help you. I can't even protect you in the locker room anymore. All a dragon's good for is burning things down."

"We're not burning anything down. We're building things up."

"You can do whatever you want. I'm staying out of it."

"Odin Thompson, *you are not a coward.*"

He looks at me.

I blow the hair out of my eyes. "I can't do this by myself. I need you. This is something we can only do together."

Now it's Odin's turn to look like he's bungee jumping without a net. Maybe we can take the plunge together. "What's the idea?"

I take a deep breath. "Let's subdue the enemy without fighting."

One grand scheme explanation later, and there's a lot of shaking heads (from him) and shaky hands (from me), but in the end, he says, "You sure this is going to work?"

"No. But I'm sure it's worth trying."

"So," Odin says, "we can sketch and paint six portraits in three hours, without stopping. That's an average of a new portrait every half hour."

"Right."

"If we work on this together every day for three hours a day, from today until Thursday, that's fifteen hours of work. And thirty paintings."

"Plus the two portraits of us."

"Thirty-two."

"Right."

"You know what carpal tunnel is?"

"We can take breaks."

"What about our homework?"

"We can get it done later at night."

"We could really get into trouble."

"It'll be worth it."

Odin narrows his eyes. "You're committed to this."

I brush the hair out of mine. "I want to change the world."

He looks away. "This is a big risk. What's happening with you and Ron . . . I've been there. I don't want to go there again." He hugs his stomach tightly. It looks like he's thinking about whatever happened in his past, letting it splash against his legs like the remnants of a tsunami. "I don't want to get hurt again," he whispers. "There are too many Rons in the world and not enough people like you."

"Do you think we can't do it?"

"Yes. I think we can't do it. If we try, I'll be destroyed. *We'll* be destroyed. Again. You think the world is a fundamentally good place, but it's not."

"I don't think that," I say, whispering too. "Everyone

has good and bad in them, and I think everyone is capable of being good if they try."

"Wouldn't that mean everyone is capable of being bad too?"

"Yeah. Which means you need to give people opportunities to be good instead of opportunities to be bad. I believe we can do it, Odin. But I can't do it without you."

He curls into a ball, knees squeezed against his chest, eyes pressed tightly shut. What am I doing to him? I can't make him relive his trauma. "If you want to back out, I totally understand," I say.

"No," he whispers. "I'll . . . I'll do it. I trust you. Even if I don't believe in humanity, I still believe in you."

He trusts me. He *believes in me.*

Odin wheels his chair to his desk, shaking his head to clear away the demons. "Who are we starting with?" he asks.

"Ron."

My friend sits up straight. "Why?"

I speak slowly. "Because he needs to learn, maybe more than anyone."

Odin sighs. "This better work." He sets the egg timer and starts sketching.

"You don't have anything for me?" I ask.

"I've been blocked. You can read a book if you want."

That statement floors me. I know how protective

Odin is with his books. "I'm good for now."

Odin goes to work sketching Ron's hairline, chin, and ears. (I give him special instructions for this picture, which he follows to the letter.) He's a fast sketcher, very efficient with how he does line work. The way his hand moves across the parchment, the way his fingers grip the pencil, the way his dark, intense eyes zoom into the page with laser focus, the way his—

Oh no.

Oh no no no no no.

My heart is thudding out of my chest once I succumb to the weight of a thousand truth bricks. I like Odin.

I like Odin.

Was it that obvious to everyone but me? Was it obvious to *him*?

But—but he might not even be gay. All that stuff about "if it was a date" could have been friend talk. He's "been there" with bullies, but that doesn't necessarily mean it was because he's gay. Maybe I've been completely misreading things. But what if I haven't been? What if he's gay? Not only that, but what if he—what if he—

"What are you doing? You're breathing loud."

Oh craaaaaaaap. "N-Nothing."

Odin looks up from his sketch. "You're all red. Are you sick? I don't want you bringing germs in here."

"I'm fine. But I-I think I should—I should g-go."

"Huh?" Odin squints. "Why? What about the enthigacs?"

"M-Maybe another day. I remembered something I, uh, had to do, some laundry, left the oven on, hahaha, it was nice being here, thanks for—"

I stand up and trip and fall flat on my face.

Odin grabs my hands and tries pulling me up, but I try to stay on the floor, it's much safer down here. "What's the matter with you?" he growls, yanking me to my feet—

—and my face comes up about three inches from his.

My ears seal up and all I can hear is the blood pumping through me. He's not moving his face away and I can smell brown sugar on his breath and I feel like I'm drowning in those deep ravines of eyes he has. "Um, Odin," I squeak.

The next thing I know his lips brush against mine. It's only for a split second, but they leave behind autumn and softness and a roaring, raging inferno in the core of my belly. Everything is tingly and everything is somehow both impossibly foggy and as clear as anything has ever been and ever will be.

Then Odin drops me and I fall back to the carpet, banging my head on his bedpost.

The sudden, jarring change and ache in my head makes me let out the loudest swear word I've ever uttered, so loud that Mr. Thompson has to knock on the door and ask, "Are you boys okay in there?"

"Yes!" Odin cries, panic and frenzy in the word.

Once Mr. Thompson's footsteps disappear down the stairs, I rub my head and look at Odin, who is more nervous, more fidgety, more *human* than I've ever seen him look. He isn't making eye contact with me.

I try to control my breathing, which, if Odin thought it was loud before, now you can probably hear it up the street. "Um," I say, my voice sounding like a soprano's, "what was that?"

Odin looks out his window, away from me. "That was a kiss," he whispers.

"Oh," I breathe, even though that's not really what I meant, and I'm sure Odin knows that.

Odin looks like he's having a wrestling match with himself, and both sides are getting pinned to the mat. "Did you . . . uh . . ."

Did I what? Did I want to leave? Did I want to get back to work? Did I never want to speak to him again?

"Did you like it?"

I can't help it: I laugh. Not just laugh, I crack up, roaring laughter that cascades out of me in waves. I roll on the floor and pound my fist in the carpet. In my tears I look up at Odin, watching me like now *I'm* the one pinning him. I try to steady myself, but then I start cracking up again. "You dropped me onto your bedpost!"

And then, Odin Thompson, in spite of his best efforts, breaks out into a grin. "Shut up," he says. "Not my fault you collapsed."

"I didn't collapse! You dropped me!"

"Whatever." Odin keeps smiling. Now that the switch is pressed, he can't turn it off.

Once I finally stop laughing, I look at Odin, and he looks at me, and I laugh *again*, and this time Odin joins in, laughing like it's a muscle he hasn't exercised in a long time. His laughs are short and choppy and listening to them is like playing in the sea at low tide.

Once we recover—for real this time—Odin gives me a very serious look. "You're not mad?"

"Why would I be mad?"

Odin considers this. If he has an answer for it, he doesn't provide one. Instead he says, "We shouldn't tell anybody about this."

Reality slowly sets back in. The rumors are bad enough, but what happens if they become true? "Okay. I guess we should get back to work."

"I guess so."

We crank out six portraits (but between you and me, it takes us a little longer than three hours). Once all is said and done, we admire our handiwork.

"I still don't know about this," Odin says.

"Me neither," I say. "But I want to problem solve through kindness."

"Kindness only gets you so far."

I smile. "Then let's reach the limits."

I wave to Odin as I climb into Mom's car, and I watch him in the rearview mirror until Mom turns and I can't see him anymore.

"Did you have a nice time?" Mom asks.

I nod.

"That's good," Mom says. "It makes me happy to see you smile."

But as we get closer and closer to 16 Werther Street, I stop smiling.

If it was a date would we keep it secret?

What would Ron do to me—to us—if he found out? If Odin's been down this road before, if that's the source of his scars, how can I drag him down it again? Or is he coming along willingly? And my identity as a gay kid can't always come first; there's more to me than that. But if I can let my identity as an artist run free, would that solve everything? Or would that make it worse?

I've learned better than to ask, *What's the worst that could happen?* because inevitably something worse than the worst does. I've also learned better than to use reverse psychology and ask, *What's the best that could happen?* because that can result in something worse than the worse than the worst. So instead I'm simply going to ask, *What is going to happen?* That seems harmless enough. I don't know what is going to happen. All I know is I'm rapidly approaching that crossroads Miss Richter warned me about—and I better pay attention to where I cross.

TWENTY-ONE

That night at dinner Dad tells us the good news. "Your mother and I will be chaperoning the dance."

I choke on my water. "Huh?"

"Harrison Money Group is sponsoring, so Mr. Harrison will be there. It'll look good for us to be there as well."

Oh great. Just what I wanted: Dad to hover around my neck, capturing all my awkward preteen moments standing around watching other people have fun. Mom looks about as thrilled as I do.

Dad turns to Nathan. "Unfortunately for you, Friday was the last day for selling tickets."

Nathan leans back in his chair. "Yep. Too bad."

"Good thing I asked the faculty coordinator to hold one aside for you."

Nathan practically falls over. "I can't go to this stupid dance. I don't have a date."

"I can be your date," Mom says with an awkward giggle.

My brother looks like he wants to bury his head in a pile of sand. I think he wants to bury some people too.

Dad massages his temples. "This is the most important time for all of us. After I get this promotion, things will be so much easier for everyone."

"We'll have more money to pay for the art academy and the engineering workshop," Mom says.

Dad nods. "We all have to buckle down and do our jobs. Alan, June will still be there, so you'd better be on your best behavior. Dance with her a lot."

"I don't dance. And June doesn't want to dance with me."

"Like I said," Dad says, "we all have to buckle down and do our jobs. Your job isn't to be an artist. Your job is to be a good kid and listen to me. Unless you have any other secret applications to programs that are total wastes of time?"

"Jimmy," Mom says. "Enough."

Dad stands up from the table and scowls at me. "You're my son. Make me proud." He heads for the garage.

At least he didn't say, "Don't disappoint me."

"Mom," Nathan whines, "I don't want to go to this

dance. Neither of us do." Nathan's been including me in subtle ways like this. Good to present a unified front against Dad, I guess.

"I know," Mom sighs. "It's only one night. It'll make your father happy."

"Nothing makes Dad happy," Nathan says. "After the dance it'll be something else. That's how it always is."

Mom reaches over the table to squeeze Nathan's hand, but he breaks away and runs upstairs, leaving her clutching air. She gathers the dishes and starts washing them.

I help her in silence, letting the cool rhythm of the faucet flood past the ticking of the clock. Drying dishes puts me in a Zen mood. It clears my head.

Dad's right: we all have to do our jobs.

"Hey, Mom?"

Mom looks up from the sink.

I hesitate, because I'm still not sure if Mom is an ally, an enemy, or something in between. But I need to know. "Hypothetically . . . if there was someone I actually wanted to go to the dance with . . ." I pause. "And they wanted to go with me too . . ."

She dries her hands off with another rag. "Do whatever makes you happy."

"Even if Dad's promotion is on the line?"

"Your father's been going on about this promotion for

over a year. I'm pretty sure it's never going to happen."

"So you'd be okay if I wanted to go with—" I can't say it. I can't bring myself to say it.

Mom places a hand on my shoulder. "Nathan's right: your father's never happy. That doesn't mean you can't be. Maybe he'll make it there someday, if you and your brother show him how." She smiles. "Wherever that happiness takes you, that's where you need to go. That's why I mailed your art academy application. And that's why you should go to the dance with—with whoever you want."

Water swims in the back of my eyes.

I give my mother a big hug and say, "Love you, Mom."

It's like she forgets how to move, like her circuits get gummed up. How long has it been since we said it? After I hold her for a few seconds, she wraps her arms around me and whispers, "Love you too. Always."

"Always?"

She squeezes deep. "*Always.*"

That night, I'm plotting the exact way I want an enthigac's smile to curve, when Nathan pokes his head inside my room. "So if I ran away from home one night and hid at Marcellus's for a week, you wouldn't say anything, would you?"

"Yeah, I guess," I mutter.

“What’s the matter with you?” Nathan asks, walking to my desk.

“Girl troubles,” I say. “Guy troubles. Dad troubles. Ron troubles. Lots of troubles.”

“Is this about the text thing?”

“That’s part of it. Nathan . . . do you think I’m too nice?”

Nathan doesn’t laugh, which surprises me. “Normally I’d say yes. But being nice works out for you. I’m sure you’ll figure out whatever crap you’re dealing with.”

“I wish I was as sure as you.”

He shrugs. “You’re like a superhero. You always find a way.” He shuts the door.

My brother called me a superhero. My brother, who used to be one of the meanest, cruelest people on the planet, told me I always find a way.

My brother believes in me.

Better not let him down.

TWENTY-TWO

From Monday to Thursday, I'm over at Odin's house working on our enthigacs. By Tuesday we've developed a rhythm, and when I leave on Thursday we've reached our goal: thirty-two paintings.

Odin's stopped asking me if I'm sure about this. I think by now he trusts me. I don't want to squander that trust.

Gladstone still hangs over our heads as we work, like one of us will let something slip about how excited we are to work with Victoria Gladstone or to meet some of the celebrities of the local art world, and there's an uncomfortable silence that always follows. But we get over it, and we keep working. We don't talk about how the academy is only held every three years. He doesn't tell me what he submitted in his application, whether it was a dragon picture, a portrait, or something else. I don't tell him how much my heart aches to go because I know he feels the same way.

"Hey," I say to Odin on Thursday, the day before the dance, as we sketch and paint. "About the dance."

He doesn't look up.

"I've been thinking."

He sketches dutifully, not making eye contact.

"And maybe . . . maybe I'd like to go with you."

He stops sketching, but he still doesn't look up at my glow-in-the-dark blush. "Ron will probably be there."

"Yeah." He has to be, for my big plan to work.

"Your parents too. And they don't know."

I gulp.

He hesitates, then goes back to sketching. I sigh, then go back to painting.

After a few seconds, he breaks the silence. "If Ron stayed out of our business . . . and your dad didn't have a heart attack . . . then maybe . . . I wouldn't mind going with you either."

My heart takes a great leap. "Yeah?"

"Yeah."

I fumble over the words. The ability to do anything vocal cord–related seems to have fled my body. But I don't think saying anything is necessary. This is a silence that speaks.

We finish the enthigacs, but it doesn't feel triumphant at all. I don't tell Odin this, but I've been losing confidence in this plan as the days have gone by. It seems so far-fetched. Am I being too nice?

Odin walks me to the door and says, "I hope it's worth it," and gives me a peck on the lips.

And I realize, just like that, it's already been worth it.

But I can't think about that now (which is really, really hard not to do, let me tell you). I've got to focus on the enthigacs. We chose the subjects carefully; it involved a lot of paying attention to other parts of the massive, congested school that we normally weren't privy to. We even snuck into different grades' lunch periods to get a firsthand account of the social ladder among the eighth and ninth graders. Plus Nathan was helpful when it came to talking about his own grade. Hopefully it's enough research to make sure we get it right.

Since I let Zack and Madison in on the secret, they've been asking me for updates all week, waiting for the reveal. I've put them to work too, and they've both been more than eager to help when the big day comes.

There's one more person I've had to let in on the secret. Our class president was more than happy to finally "see some social change happen around here"—even if it means breaking the rules.

When Talia MacDonald is okay with breaking the rules, you know it's serious.

Friday. The day of the Winter Dance.

I leave 16 Werther Street before anyone's awake and hop on my bike. The cold December air fills my lungs, even as I'm bundled up with a hat, gloves, and a scarf. As I start the trek to Evergreen, a light dusting of snow falls, coating the grass and roads with a fine, white powder. It wasn't supposed to snow today. Five minutes into my bike ride, and things are already going wrong. I ignore that little voice of doubt and pedal to my middle school, my breath puffing out in clouds before my face. My eye is fully healed. I'm not the face of bullying at Evergreen anymore. I'm not the face of anything. I'm just the receptacle for my art, and, regardless of what Odin says about art vs. artists, that art's about to change the world.

I'm the second to show up at Evergreen; Talia's already there, a grim determination in her eyes. Soon after, Madison arrives, red face hidden behind a thick jacket. Zack bikes up hot on his heels. "Morning," he says with a yawn. "Why haven't we started yet?"

"Odin has the paintings," I say.

Talia rubs her hands together. "Are you sure he's coming?"

"I trust him."

We wait a minute. And another. And another. I check my phone. No texts. If Odin doesn't show up with those paintings, the whole thing falls apart. Maybe he's not showing up. Maybe he hates me and he's never going to speak to me again and the whole enthigac operation is ruined and I'm a terrible human being and—

"We should at least go inside," Madison says.

"The plan said to meet by the bike rack," I say, ignoring how hoarse my voice sounds. "He'll be here."

"If Alan says he'll be here, then he'll be here," Zack says. He tries to catch a snowflake on his tongue.

After about five minutes, when I'm this close to texting Odin, his bike appears in the distance. I wave my arms around to get his attention, fighting the urge to run up to him and hug him to death.

"Sorry I'm late," Odin says, out of breath. "I had to convince my dad to let me bike here by myself."

"Do you have the paintings?" Talia asks.

Odin pats his backpack.

"Then let's go," she says.

We move around to a side entrance of the building, to a trash door that, according to Talia, is always unlocked. "This is disgusting," Madison says, wrinkling his nose as we pass the dumpster. "When was the last time someone did a garbage pickup out here?"

"Quit whining," Talia says.

"I am *not* whining. I'm stating an objection in a forceful manner."

"That's whining."

"You wouldn't know the first thing about—"

"Guys!" I say. "Come on."

It feels so strange to be here around six in the morning, before the first buses arrive. School starts at seven fifteen, and there are teachers creaking around their classrooms, so we need to be extra cautious. The distant drone of the heat and other electronics fills the building with an eerie calm, one that could be snapped shut at any moment.

We make our way to the gym/pool area, which is where the dance is going to be held tonight. Talia disappears for a second with Zack and Odin, leaving Madison and me blowing warm breath onto our hands. The three of them reappear clutching small ladders. "The janitor's closet by the gym is always unlocked," Talia says, proudly lifting her head up.

"I could have told you that," Madison grumbles.

"What about the camera?" I gesture to the black circle in the corner of the hall.

"Nobody mans the security office until six thirty," Talia says. "We're fine."

"One of the coaches could come out of the gym area anytime," Madison says.

"Nobody goes in or out of the gym or pool until roughly six seventeen every day, when Coach Streit walks into her office with a cup of coffee."

Zack hums. "Nice detective work."

"It's what any good class president would do," Talia says.

Odin opens his bag and spreads the paintings on the ground. Talia adjusts her glasses. "Not bad. You did all this in a week?"

"Five days," Odin says.

Zack picks one up and shows it to Madison. "I like this one."

Madison stares at it hypnotically. "You captured my smile."

"Thanks," I say.

"I wore Officer Orville Orange today," Zack says with a grin, lifting his shirt to show the waistband of my old, bright orange, lucky underwear. "Remember him, Alan?"

Odin shoots me an odd look. "Uh, long story," I say, cheeks flushing at the pair of tighty-orangies I gave

Zack as one of the challenges in Nathan's last game of CvC. "Come on, we've got to hurry."

"Wait," Odin says. "I just want to say . . ." He hesitates. "Let's kick ass."

"Yeah!" Zack pumps his fist.

It occurs to me then, as we set up the ladders, that we're actually doing this. We're setting things into motion. We're putting art into people's minds. We're trying to change the world.

I set up a ladder at one end of the hall and start taping my stack of paintings to the wall, high above the lockers. Odin works across from me. Talia starts at the other end of the hall, and across from her, Zack sits on Madison's shoulders to reach above the lockers.

It takes us ten minutes to hang everything, with more than enough time to be done before Coach Streit shows up. The five of us, all yawning and stretching, stop to admire our handiwork: thirty-two paintings, hanging high above in the hall where the largest number of people can see them. I smile at Odin. "Feels good, huh?"

Odin tries to rub the sleep out of his eyes. "We'll see what happens next."

Within forty-five minutes most of the buses arrive. The five of us wait in Miss Richter's room, listening for any signs of disturbance. I pace around the back of the classroom. Zack keeps flitting in and out of the room. Finally, I say, "I can't take it anymore. I've got to check it out."

"I'm coming with you," Odin says.

So we make the trek down to the gym area, passing by a number of dance decorations throughout the hall: tinsel, banners, paper snowflakes. As we approach the pool, we stop. There's a crowd gathered.

A large crowd.

We elbow into the throng of kids—and teachers—who are stopping and admiring our paintings. "Where did these come from?" someone asks.

"Hey, that's me!" Bryce Garrett, a big, tough ninth grader, says, pointing at a picture with emotionally vulnerable eyes. "What the crap? I don't look like that!"

"I know that girl," someone else says, motioning toward a painting with shiny auburn hair. "Whoever did these did a great job with the colors."

"This is stupid," a loud girl says. "They're taking up all this space."

"No, they're not," someone else says. "They're so high up, you barely even notice them."

"Who painted me?" Bryce keeps thundering. "Who gave me those stupid, girly eyes? That's not cool!"

The bell is about to ring, and the crowd shows no

signs of parting. We rush back to homeroom. I look at Odin. "Well?"

"The world hasn't changed yet," he says.

We make it right before the bell. Miss Richter watches us carefully as we sit down, keen eyes taking us in.

Connor leans over to me and whispers, "I heard there's a painting of you hanging by the gym."

"Yeah, there's pictures of Alan and Madison and Odin," Sheila says.

Zack shrugs, a goofy grin on his face. "That's neat."

I smile. "Yeah. That's neat."

"Hush," Miss Richter says, barely able to hide a smile.

The morning announcements begin. "Would the following students please report to the principal's office: Talia MacDonald, Alan Cole, Madison Truman, Odin Thompson, and Zachary Kimble. *Immediately.*"

My stomach plummets. This was always a possibility though, and I'm prepared for it. Let's hope I don't screw it up.

"Ooh, the principal's office," Zack says as we all walk over. "I've never been inside before. I heard there's an aquarium. Do you think Principal Dorset will let us see the aquarium?"

Madison is running his hands over his hair so much they're leaving messy strands behind—which is impressive, since Madison has a buzz cut. "I can't go to the office. When my parents find out, they'll disown me. Oh, I should never have agreed to this. Why did you let me agree to this?"

"Be quiet," Talia says, leading the way. "Alan Cole has a plan. Isn't that right?"

I gulp. "Yeah. That's right."

The five of us pack into Principal Dorset's office like sardines. There is no aquarium, but Zack amuses himself by trying to follow the blades on the ceiling fan. "So," the principal says to us. "What do you have to say for yourselves?"

"About what?" Talia asks.

"You know what," Principal Dorset says. "Hanging unauthorized decorations in the halls. Not any decorations—representations of students! Hanging without their permission. This is a very serious offense."

"Eep," Madison gurgles.

Odin, propped against the wall, arms crossed, keeps silent. If he's feeling anything underneath that stoic mask of a face, he's not letting on.

"Principal Dorset," Talia presses on, "what proof do you have it was us?"

"The security camera."

"That's preposterous," Talia says. "Nobody uses the security office until six thirty and we finished hanging the pictures at six ten, six twelve at the latest."

Odin facepalms.

"We started a new security schedule this week," Principal Dorset says. "The only reason the guard didn't stop you was because he was chatting with a few teachers and not monitoring the feed. Suffice to say he'll think twice about being social when children are running rampant around the school."

"Oh," Talia says in a small voice. Madison looks like he's about to wet himself.

"The guard identified the five of you hanging these papers. With unauthorized usage of school equipment as well! Ladders are not for children."

"Principal Dorset—"

"That's enough, Talia. I was hoping I'd seen the last of you in my office back in October, after your offensive school debate performance. The same for you, Alan. It's clear you've both roped unwitting accomplices into your act this time. I won't stand for it. Vandalism and rule breaking to an unheard of degree!" He sits back and rubs his temples.

I take a deep breath. "W-Well, Principal Dorset, there's a little more to it than that."

Principal Dorset opens his eyes. "Oh?"

I plunge forward. "This whole thing was an art project me and Odin decided to do. After I got . . . beat up,

I wanted to take a stand against bullying. I've always been a big believer that art can change the world." I can almost feel Odin rolling his eyes at me. "So I, uh, I thought that by painting the faces of people who'd either been bullied or were bullies, it might, uh, show people a more human side of things. It would put faces to the whole thing."

Principal Dorset says nothing, which is my cue to continue.

"We wanted to paint honest pictures. For the kids who get bullied, we tried to show their inner strength and courage. For the bullies, we wanted to show their soft side, their vulnerability. This is our enthigac."

"Your ethno-what?"

"Enthigac. It's an anagram for 'change it.'" I breathe deep. "Sun Tzu said 'the supreme art of war is to subdue the enemy without fighting.' That means be prepared. Make the enemy accept your demands before you even start the battle. You can do both of those things through understanding your opponent. You can even, instead of fighting, problem solve through kindness. That's what we wanted to do."

Principal Dorset leans back in his chair. "Sun Tzu."

"Miss Richter made us read him," Zack chimes in.

"I've got to have a word with her about the ASPEN curriculum," the principal mutters. "What do you think this . . . ethno-gack is going to specifically accomplish?"

"We hope kids will look at our paintings, and feel a connection to the people inside them, and maybe change their behavior because of it. There's no such thing as a world without bullying. We know that. But if we can make a world with less of it, even a little less, then we'll have done our part."

The principal considers this. "Did you have to hang these right before the dance?"

"Especially right before the dance," I say.

"Also," Talia says, "we didn't go around the decorations committee. The class presidents are technically in charge of all the dance subcommittees, so I was simply exerting my executive powers. In case you were concerned about that."

Principal Dorset lets out a deep sigh. "Does anyone else have anything to say?"

"Where's your aquarium?" Zack asks. "Do you only show it to the good students?"

"I, er, ah," Madison stammers out. "I've been bullied. A lot. I'm happy my face is up there. And I'm proud to do my part." He puffs out his chest.

Principal Dorset looks at Odin, who nods. Just a nod. That's enough.

We watch our principal lean forward in his chair, elbows rested on his table, for a while. The only noise, apart from Madison's breathing, is from the central heat, and it's starting to feel pretty hot in here, all right.

Finally, after giving the matter what feels like fifteen hours' worth of consideration, Principal Dorset grabs his intercom and says, "Good morning, Evergreen. I apologize for disrupting your classes, but I wanted to bring your attention to the new decorations lining the hall outside our gym and pool."

Whoa.

"They were painted by two of our Saplings in an attempt to shed light on bullying. If you see your picture in the halls and you do not wish it to be there, speak with a teacher and we will remove it for you. Otherwise, enjoy the artistic talents of Alan Cole and Odin Thompson—as well as their ambitious desire to change the world." He puts the intercom away.

I'm too stunned to say anything. It's like Batman showed up to offer me a ride in the Batmobile, and the Batmobile had soda and cookies. But better. "Principal Dorset," Talia says, sounding every bit as stunned as I feel, "you won't regret—"

Principal Dorset holds up a hand. "Have fun at the dance, children."

By the time I get to swimming, the enthigacs are all anyone is talking about. Which is nice, because it means people aren't talking about the "Alan totally frenched Odin" rumor anymore. No, now we're in the spotlight for a different reason. A better reason.

In the locker room, Ron taunts, "Look at the little artist with his stupid pictures."

"God, Ron, shut up," Jamal Lawrence mutters.

"Surprised there's no picture of you up there," someone says.

"Why would there be?" Ron asks. "I'm not a bully."

I don't say anything. Ron has an enthigac all right—but it's not hanging outside the pool.

Odin joins me once I'm done changing.

"Look at this," Ron sneers. "Off to suck face some more?"

Odin's been quiet since the week began, back when the rumors were flying faster than a seagull over Trash Island. But now he breaks his silence. "You," he says to Ron, loud enough that the whole locker room can hear, "are a coward."

Ron snorts. "Sure. Tell yourself that so you can sleep easier."

"You'll see," Odin says. We walk off together.

"I don't need a lecture from a couple of homos!" Ron calls out.

"Shut up, Ron," Jamal says.

We round the corner and, when no one is looking, Odin squeezes my hand.

I practically jump out of my shoes. Then, when no one is looking, I squeeze back. Our hands separate and our arms fall to the side, but we both walk a little taller to our next classes.

Enthigacs show the world the way you're afraid to look at it. Like how my and Odin's portraits are facing each other. Or how Madison's face is sweaty, like pleasing people every day is an effort. Whether artists or their art are the ones doing the changing, all I know is: change has come to Evergreen Middle School.

Now let's see if change has come to Alan Cole.

TWENTY-THREE

I've never seen the parking lot at Evergreen any fuller. Cars are practically bursting out onto the street. After around ten minutes of driving past full row after full row, Dad gives up and parks on a street a few blocks away, grumbling the whole time. We can hear the pounding music from our space.

We're all dressed up pretty nicely—Dad's wearing a button-up with a tie, Mom's got a nice, crisp dress, and me and Nathan are wearing white dress shirts with very sharp (so I've been assured) ties. Dad made my brother put gel in his hair, and he keeps trying to press it out in between his fingers, which only makes him look worse.

Nathan kicks up slush as we walk the three blocks to Evergreen; otherwise we walk in silence. Of course there are kids dressed super casually, which makes me stick out like a bloated, sharp-tie-wearing thumb. That doesn't matter though. What matters is I've got a plan. A big one. It requires the right people being in the right places at the right times. We might pull it off. We might fail horribly. Either way, I'm going to attempt to take the identity I've chosen and the identity that's chosen me and combine them into something new and bold and exciting and world changing.

I'm terrified. That just means I'm doing it right.

Once we're a block away, Dad says, "The Harrisons will meet us at the entrance."

Dad still wants me and June to blossom into a happy, sunshiny, heterosexual couple, and it's not going to happen, for a wide variety of reasons. At least June was on the same page when we went to the mall, though she's so chaotic she might have changed her mind by now. I need to find June, I need to find Odin, I need to find Ron, and I need to find Connor—in that order.

As we approach the entrance, full of teens smoking on the steps, June bounds up to me, wearing a black dress with what looks like a flower in her hair. "Good evening," she says.

I nod. "Hi."

Mr. Harrison gives Dad and Mom a big greeting, then turns to me. "Hello again, Mr. Roadkill."

"Uh—"

"Do I need to search you for rats?" When I physically take a step back from Dad's very tall and very imposing boss, he laughs. "Relax. Bygones, eh? You kids have fun tonight."

Mom looks at me with worry etched on her forehead, but she follows Dad, who looks back at me with eyes of clear warning and trails Mr. Harrison, who proceeds to tell some of the smokers about how unhealthy nicotine is.

"Okay. Bye, Daddy. See you later." June wrenches herself free from the watchful eye of her father and yanks me up the steps, Nathan following behind. When she reaches the top, she pulls the corsage out of her hair and tosses it into the bushes. "Ugh. Adults."

"I hear you."

"I guess we're supposed to go in there and have a good time or something."

"Supposedly." Go for it, Alan. Time to see if she really is your friend. "But I had something else in mind."

We walk into Evergreen. "Go on," she says.

Nathan surges up from behind us. "Okay. You guys have fun. I'm going to slink into a corner and try not to choke on my own puke."

"Save some for me," June calls as Nathan runs off. Then, to me, "You know I'm always up for mischief."

"It's not exactly mischief. I'll show you."

The lights inside Evergreen are dimmed, but it's easy to tell where the dance is being held by the thumping bass. The farther into the school we get, the more people are clustering in the halls, being watched over by bored-looking adults. Once we're in the hall outside the gym, there are groups of people admiring the enthigacs, which fills me with a warm sensation not unlike the summer's first bite of cotton candy. There are a couple of empty spaces in the rows of paintings, which means kids requested to have their pictures removed. But most of them are still up.

"I'm guessing you're responsible for this," June says, gesturing to the enthigacs.

"Something like that."

June considers the paintings. "Not bad. Not exactly typical dance decoration though." She eyes up my own enthigac, the one Odin started of me, facing the one I started of Odin, but she doesn't comment on it. "Is this what you want me for? To pose for a painting? I'm flattered."

"Not quite. Do you remember the guy we met at the mall?"

"How could I ever forget such a darling specimen."

"He's probably here. I need to give him one of these paintings. But if I try to talk to him, it'll just turn into a shouting match or—something worse."

June sighs. "Alan, Alan, Alan. Just because I like you doesn't mean I'm magically a good person. What possible reason would there be for me to help you talk to this clown?"

"Because you said you were my friend?"

"I'm not only a bad person, I'm a bad friend too. Who knew?"

"Well, I don't need you to help me talk to him. I need a way to get him to notice me."

"Like a distraction?"

I nod.

June's face slowly spreads into a wide, candy cane–shaped grin. "I guess I'll be earning my friendship bracelet after all."

"There are rules. Nobody gets hurt and nothing gets seriously damaged."

"But those are the best parts!"

"June."

She laughs. "So serious. Just like your dad."

Ew! I suddenly feel the need to take a shower.

"Fine. I, June Harrison, will help my best friend of all time, Alan Cole, by causing widespread mayhem and panic. So it is decreed, so it is done."

After I explain to June what exactly I need—and after I emphasize again how "widespread mayhem and panic" is not meant to be taken literally—she smiles.

"This is some plan. You're putting yourself in the cross-hairs for something that might not even work."

Not just me. "I'm willing to take the risk."

"I can see that. Text me when you're in position, and I'll make it happen. Ooh, I'm so excited! You have no idea."

"Thanks for doing this."

"No. Thank you. This will only make the next time we fight even sweeter." She rubs her hands together and waltzes toward the gym, bobbing her head to the beat. She stops when she reaches the entrance. "Alan?"

"Yeah?"

When June Harrison looks back at me, there's—for the briefest of moments—a real person standing there, trying to break free. She smiles an earnest, genuine smile. Then she regains control and says, "Try not to die out there."

I gulp.

Step one: complete. Now to find Odin. I check up and down the hallway and inside the bathroom, so the only place left for him to be is—gulp—the gym.

I steady myself and, my body rigid as a plank of wood, enter the dance floor.

Wow. It's *huge.* The whole gym has been turned into a strobetastic display, and—this is what gets me—the wall between the gym and the pool has disappeared, and the bleachers have been folded up, and the pool has been sealed off. They put some metal covering over the pool and it's gone! Just like that!

Of course, I can barely focus on these thoughts because the music—some pop song about shaking your butt—is overwhelming and all the people make it impossible for me to breathe without hitting someone.

"Hey, Alan!" someone yells. Meredith Wood is standing there, looking like she's not having too much of a blast herself. "Have you seen Madison?"

"I haven't seen him!" I yell.

She puts a hand over her ear. "What?"

"I don't know where he is!"

"Huh?"

I shake my head. There's no point in talking. My voice box doesn't have a setting that loud.

Meredith frowns. Now that I know she doesn't like me, her little gestures take on new meaning. "If you see him, let him know I'm looking for him. Okay?"

Zack has a spot on the floor all to himself, doing what I can only assume is that ludicrous Zack Shuffle. He's so focused on shimmying his hips that he trips onto his face. Oh well, he seems like he's having fun. He's on security detail for the plan. When the signal goes out, he's supposed to make sure Ron doesn't go astray. If I can trust anyone in the world to watch my back, it's Zack Kimble.

Meredith watches this display with her nose in the air, then walks away.

Good luck, Madison. You'll need it.

A new song comes on, which I'm pretty sure is some sort of trendy dance number I've overheard on the radio that uses the word "baby" every five seconds. Zack dances his Shuffle, and now it looks like a crowd is forming around him, possibly out of sheer befuddlement.

Still no Odin.

Maybe he didn't come after all; maybe the plan intimidated him too much. I didn't text him to meet me anywhere—I guess I was a little shy—but now I wish I had. I try to navigate past the hurricane of kids only to get blown in the wrong direction, and now I'm in front of Connor and Sheila, grinding like a violin and its bow. Before I can squeeze away, Connor notices me. "Hey, Alan!" he shouts. "Having fun, man?"

"The panda eats cheese in an igloo!"

He puts a hand to his ear. "Huh?"

I sigh. I need to find Odin and Ron before Connor. This plan doesn't work if things happen out of order!

Then Connor reaches out and grabs my arm and yells, "Dude, you should dance with us! I'll teach you the moves if you don't know."

My heart almost shoots out of my throat. Dance with Connor?

No. It's not my dream anymore. But it's still really, really hard to back away from him, and it makes it seem like it's going to be that much harder to pull off the plan tonight now. Why couldn't Connor be a jerk like Ron? Or why couldn't he be totally nice like he was before? Why does he have to be both?

I somehow find a deserted corner of the dance floor, with various older kids too cool to bust a move hanging out. I text to Odin:

are you here? june's on standby. I know where connor is but not ron.

Seconds later my phone buzzes:

Hey

where are you?

Don't look behind you

There he is.

"I said don't look behind you," he yells.

"There you are," I yell.

He puts a hand over his ear.

I drag him out of the dance floor to the hall, with its more acceptable volume level for introverts.

Odin's dressed in his standard colorfully designed jean jacket. I adjust my tie self-consciously. "You sure Ron's coming?" Odin asks.

"No," I admit. "But if I know him, he'll want to be here to show how manly he is. He'll probably try dancing with any girl he sees. When Connor sees him though . . ." I shudder. Connor didn't ban Ron from coming to the dance or anything, but he's been waiting for the perfect moment to strike at Ron, and the dance seems like a great opportunity.

As I take a drink, someone whispers, "Is she gone?"

"No," I say to Madison, crouching by the side of the water fountain. "You need to tell her you don't want to dance."

"I can't," he says. He's wearing a blazer, tie, and dress slacks, which I can't tell if his parents forced him to wear or if it was his choice. "I don't want to hurt her feelings."

"But you don't want to be here with her."

"Yes." He exhales. "I know. I need to suck it up and do the right thing and—and break that girl's heart. What's going on with the plan?"

"Wait for the signal, then make sure Connor heads for the right place."

"Do you really expect this to work?"

"I'm willing to try."

"Well, I'll be there with you. Here's hoping Meredith doesn't disintegrate me first. You can blow my ashes in your direction and hope they get in Ron's eyes."

Madison wanders back into the pool area, looking like a lost puppy that's been asked to gnaw off its own leg. But if I can trust anyone *else* in the world to watch my back, it's Madison Wilson Truman.

Odin looks like he wants to object, like he's still not sure why we're going out of our way to do this for Ron. But that objection is quickly replaced with fidgeting and eyes darting from one end of the hall to the next. "Are your parents here?"

I nod. "We don't have to do this if you don't want to. There's still time to back out."

"No there's not. Backing out hasn't been an option since the text rumor. Probably earlier than that. It's all been leading up to this."

My nerves tingle and my brain goes on high alert, and my knees feel like they're turning to strawberry jam and this plan all of a sudden seems a lot more complicated and likelier to fail now than it did when we came up with it. But this is the final act of the enthigacs. Odin's right: the time for backing out is over.

We stand in the hall, pointedly not looking at each other, when the next song comes on. It's "Stairway to Heaven."

"Really?" Odin asks.

"Guess it's technically a slow song," I say. Then, sounding much braver than I feel, I ask, "Shall we dance?"

He nods. "Let's do it."

TWENTY-FOUR

"All right, guys and gals," the DJ booms out from somewhere in the mists, "grab a partner and take it reeeeeal sloooooow."

I have no idea why this Led Zeppelin classic rock song, which admittedly has a slow tempo at first, is considered slow dance material. But I'm not in charge of the Winter Dance song selection committee. If I were, there would be a lot more class and a lot less bass (I know that doesn't rhyme, just let me have this).

Odin and I make our way to the poolside, passing by lots of couples doing that awkward middle school arm's-length hold thing. All hetero couples. We find a spot on one of the slabs covering the pool. I take out my phone, hand shaking like I've downed three cups of coffee, and text June:

we're on top of the pool. ready.

We look at each other, neither of us wanting to make the first move. ("Stairway to Heaven" is a long song, but it's not so long that we can stand around all day.) Odin is the first to act, placing one hand on my waist and the other on my shoulder. I follow suit.

And we dance.

Well, sort of. I don't know if you can really call the middle school arm's-length hold thing dancing. But we sway to the music, looking anywhere but at each other, just like all the other couples swaying around us.

"Do you have any idea what this song means?" I ask. The lack of thumping bass means people can hear me.

Odin shakes his head. "Not a clue."

And people begin to notice us. Some of the couples pull away from our dance spot, but some give us smiles and encouraging nods.

I trip over Odin's foot and almost plunge into his shoulder.

A voice comes over the microphone:

"Would Ronnie McCaughlin please come to the pool area? Ronnie, you are needed on top of the pool. That's little Ronnie McCaughlin, to the pool. Thank you. Have a great night everybody! Tip your waitress!"

Everyone looks around confused.

"How did she do that?" Odin asks.

I shrug. "She's June Harrison. She finds a way." Step two: complete.

The singer from Led Zeppelin croons about forests and hedges or something. We sway.

"This really isn't a good slow song," Odin says.

"Better this then some sappy ballad."

"Is it?"

"Good point."

"Hey!"

The cry cuts through the music. Odin's hands squeeze into me, either reflexively or protectively.

Ron stomps through the crowd to us, which parts to let him through. We don't move. Zack follows slightly behind him.

"Well, well, well," Ron sneers, walking closer and closer. "You had to come here and show off your homo crap to everyone, didn't you?"

We stare him down.

Ron's voice reaches the ceiling. "You're lucky there's a million people here, otherwise I—"

"Otherwise you'd what?" Connor asks, cutting through the crowd. Madison squeezes through the throng of people, right behind Connor. Sheila hangs back, away from the action.

Steps three and four: complete. If June had also paged Connor to the pool, Ron wouldn't have come, so we had to take the chance that Connor would want to intercept Ron. And we had to take the chance that Ron would lash out if he saw Odin and me dancing. Zack and Madison were on standby in case either Ron or Connor decided to break away from the expected route. Now for the big moment. This is it. No backing out. I say, in my loudest voice, "Ron . . . Connor . . . we have—"

"Alan Michael Cole!"

Hands forcibly pry Odin and me apart from each other. We try to hold on, but my father is too strong. "What the *hell* do you think you're doing?" he gasps.

Step five: the hardest step. "Dancing," I say, staring down the flames. "With my date."

Dad looks at Odin like Odin turned neon green and barfed lima beans on Dad's loafers. "You've got to be kidding me," he grumbles.

Mom reaches Dad's side, fingers running along her cross, and Mr. Harrison appears by my parents' side, watching the scene. Mom meets my eyes, and I don't look away and she doesn't either. Dad's face bulges from his skull like it's about to pop off. My hands, returned to Odin's shoulder and waist, shake even more furiously. Odin's trembling too; his hands squeeze into me to keep from dissolving.

By now the rest of the crowd has given everyone—me, Odin, Ron, Connor, Zack, Madison, and my parents—a wide berth.

"We're leaving," Dad thunders.

"Not yet," I say.

"I said we're *leaving*," Dad repeats. He moves to position himself in between me and Odin, but then Nathan appears, standing in front of us.

"Back off," Nathan says.

Dad looks so thrown by his eldest son's defiance that he physically takes a step back. He turns to Mr. Harrison for guidance, but his boss only shrugs.

Nathan's gesture wasn't part of the plan. He saw that I was in trouble and came to my aid, unprompted, against Dad. Against *Dad*. He turns to me and says, "Do what you need to do, Alan."

Odin and I break apart, still shaking. I look at Dad, breathing like he's swum an Olympic-sized pool. "We have something to give Ron," I say.

Ron's eyes move between me, Odin, and Connor, but his body is locked in place.

"Try it," Connor says. "I'll beat the snot out of you, you lousy—"

"And," I interrupt, "we have something to give to Connor too."

"Huh?" Connor stops.

"I don't want anything from you, homo!" Ron barks. "I'm out of here."

Ron starts moving away from the group.

Zack moves to stop Ron, but someone gets there first. Someone unexpected.

"Excuse me," Mom says.

"Out of my way," Ron grunts, trying to squeeze past.

"My son has a gift for you," Mom says. "I suggest you take it."

Mom looks unlike I've ever seen her before. Her eyes burn, but not like Dad's do sometimes—hers burn with strong desire. The desire to protect. Even Ron knows better than to get in the path of a rampaging mother.

By now no one nearby is dancing (or swaying, or whatever). Madison and Zack reach me and Odin. Their eyes take in my father, speechlessly staring at Odin, me, and Nathan; my mother, guiding Ron back into the center of the action; and Connor, watching Ron (but also me) carefully. "This is going good!" Zack chirps.

"We'll see," Madison says, on full alert.

I nod to Odin. He takes a folded-up piece of parchment paper and passes it off to me, and I pass it to Connor. Why couldn't you be all good or all bad, Connor . . . "We made you this," I say to my first crush. "You tried to do the right thing by bullying Ron, but all it did was make him hurt me more and threaten my friends. It didn't solve anything. And you . . . you actually enjoyed making him miserable."

Connor takes the enthigac of himself, eyes wide.

I continue, "Maybe you can look at what you did and change it up. You're a good guy—a *great* guy—but even great guys can become bullies if they're not careful."

Connor looks at the enthigac, then at me. "Come on, Sheila," he says to his girlfriend. "Let's go somewhere we're wanted." He leaves the crowd. And my heart breaks a little.

"Ha!" Ron laughs. "Serves you right."

"*You.*" Madison stomps forward, past me, past Odin, past everyone else, and gets into Ron's face. "Punching my best friend! Acting like you're some king of the school! Well, you're nothing but a giant homophobic jerk! Alan has treated you with nothing but kindness and you haven't deserved an ounce of it."

Mom's eyes burn a hole in Ron's face at the mention of him punching me.

"I—" Ron stammers. "I don't want his freaking charity! I just want him to go away!" No, Ron, your dad left, but I'm staying right here.

Odin hands me Ron's enthigac. Zack gives me a quick shoulder rub. Nathan hovers in between me and Dad.

June's cackle sounds in the distance, and I know she's watching too.

Dad is still staring.

All these people are in my corner (well, almost). I am filled with power, cracking the slab as I walk, lightning searing from every part of my body. No one can stop me. Not Ron. Not Dad. No one.

Ron's eyes dart around, looking for an escape, surrounded by my family and friends. I stand three feet from the boy who punched me in the face and the stomach, who kicked me when I was down, who would have done worse—so much worse—if given the opportunity. Am I too nice? Maybe. But when the world punched me in the face, I chose not to punch back.

I chose to hug the world instead.

The crowd calls things: "Kick his butt, Galan!" "Ron, what are you waiting for?" "Fight! Fight! Fight!"

We stare at each other for five seconds. Ten seconds. Twenty seconds. Ron fidgets. Squirms. Sweats. Finally, I speak. "You tried to break me. But you didn't understand. Nothing can break me. As long as I know who I am."

Ron looks down.

"When we made the enthigacs, we wanted to show people who they truly were. But with you . . . we thought it'd be better if we showed you who you could be."

I hand Ron his enthigac.

He doesn't take it at first. He looks at Mom, and she nods, and then he takes it.

His face locks into position.

Ron's enthigac is the only one with more than one person in it. The picture is of Ron, running, with his little brother on his shoulders, baseball caps at identical angles. They're both laughing. It was when I saw Ron, really saw him, that day in swimming class that I realized he never smiles when he bullies me. He acts like it's so unpleasant. That was the whole tipping point for the enthigacs. And when I saw him with Aaron, I realized he had to be capable of joy and laughter, the same as everyone else. Maybe he needed to rediscover that. Maybe he always knew, but he was afraid to show it to everyone. Maybe this can help him make peace with the "real man" his father wasn't.

He stares at his enthigac like it's going to swallow him whole.

I extend a hand to Ron for him to shake.

He looks up at me.

And he leaves.

He walks past Madison and Mom and Nathan and the rest of the crowd and keeps walking out of the pool and into the hall, and like that—just like that—he's gone.

The crowd seems disappointed that there won't be a fight, but I breathe a lot easier. Odin also exhales sharply (I wonder if he had forgotten to breathe during that whole encounter). Zack ruffles my hair, and Madison claps me on the back, and Mom gives me a big hug, in front of the whole school, and I don't even care because it fills me with such sunshine I could power an entire galaxy. Zack then hugs Odin, and Odin only resists a little bit.

Connor left though.

Because I had to be too nice.

Dad is staring. Still. Another song starts playing, this one a more upbeat number, and the crowd goes back to shimmying and shaking. But Dad just stares, like he's seeing his son anew. I walk up to him—slowly—and go to say something, but he disappears into the crowd, zombified.

"He'll come around," Nathan says.

"How do you know that?" I ask.

"I don't. I just felt like saying something reassuring."

"Alan!" Zack yells. "Come on! I'm teaching Zack Shuffle lessons! Get in on this!"

I turn to Odin. "What do you say?"

"I say, I can't believe all that plan crap worked," Odin says.

I shrug. "I get good ideas sometimes."

"Yeah. Sometimes."

June approaches the crowd surrounding Zack. "This kid is a dance disaster. My kind of party!"

Odin and I look at each other. We smile.

And we dance.

TWENTY-FIVE

The mid-December sun peeks through the clouds when I wake up one morning, the last day before the Flower County School District's winter break. The snow's been coming fast and furious the past two weeks since the Winter Dance, but we haven't had a single snow day or even an early dismissal. I'm not much for playing in the snow, but it's always nice to walk around outside in the midst of a crisp snowfall, taking in the sights.

Today, however, there's a late arrival scheduled. You'd think this means I'd be comfy in my bed, snuggled deep inside the covers, but instead I'm pacing around my room, waiting for Bill, our mailman. Today's a very important day.

Today's the day a certain art academy's rejection (or acceptance!) letters are supposed to show up.

Would you be snuggled deep inside the covers?

Once it hits nine thirty, my stomach starts mewling like a neglected kitten, so I go downstairs. Dad's at the kitchen table, with his laptop open. Ever since he finally got his promotion a week and a half ago, he's been working from home more, which means he's more of a constant presence around the house. Which sounds terrible, but he mostly does his own thing in the kitchen.

And ignores me.

Two weeks of nothing. No words, no noises, not even a quick look.

It's . . . actually been kind of nice.

And kind of not nice at the same time.

I pull up a chair and sit down, pouring myself a bowl of Lucky Charms, focused all the while on the window looking out onto the lawn, onto our lonely, snow-covered mailbox. The wooden clock ticks alongside Dad's typing. After a few half-hearted bites of marshmallows I walk to the window, thinking maybe I might have missed Bill in a spoonful of artificial flavors. I go back to the table. One spoonful after, I go back to the window.

Five trips to the window later, I sit down and resolve to at least finish my bowl of cereal before I—

"Alan."

I look up, shocked.

Without glancing up from his laptop, Dad speaks like

every word is being twisted out of him, wrung out like a wet towel. "I thought you weren't a man."

I stop chewing.

"But you stood up for yourself . . ." His hand squeezes the mouse. "In a way I can't believe. You, my goldfish."

The old nickname doesn't even hurt anymore. Doesn't even leave a mark.

"I got my promotion because I asked for it. I saw you stand up for yourself, and I realized I wasn't doing the same. You . . . showed me how it's done."

He taps his fingers along the rim of his laptop.

"I said to make me proud."

Long pause.

"Keep up the good work."

A knot in my gut unties, flaps around like a loosed bird.

"It was nice to see you happy at the dance," Dad continues. "If you want to be happy . . . I won't stop you."

I let out a tremendous breath. "Hey, Dad?"

My father looks at me for the first time in two weeks.

"You made me proud too."

He stops typing. Then he smiles. He *smiles*! My father, smiling! From a positive emotion! I expect the earth to crack open and for us to be swallowed by radioactive man-beasts. We sit together, me eating and him working, father and son.

Nathan thunders downstairs, hefty feet clonking up

the house. He just started a growth spurt, and Mom had to buy all new clothes for him. He whistles when he looks out the window. "Lots of snow. Surprised they didn't just cancel school altogether. Says it's twenty-six out. Twenty-six letters in the alphabet, but only five vowels. The capital of Mongolia is Ulaanbaatar. These pajamas were from Sears. Oh, forgot to mention, Bill's here."

I dash outside, still in my pajamas, to check the mailbox. Probably not the best idea.

"Guess I should've led with that, huh?" Nathan asks. He takes over my bowl of Lucky Charms in my absence.

As I tumble back inside, I go over the mail. Adult stuff, adult stuff, adult stuff—here it is. *Victoria Gladstone Art Academy.* I'm shivering, and it's not just from wet socks.

"Ooh, is the mail here?" Mom walks into the kitchen and asks, "Did you get your acceptance letter?"

Yeesh, no pressure there. I rip the letter open, my whole family reading over my shoulder.

Dear Alan,

So far so good.

Thank you for applying for the winter term for the Gladstone Art Academy. Unfortunately, your application was not accepted. We receive many more submissions than we can admit every term. This is especially true due to our policy of only selecting one applicant per school.

I get to the end. There's no message about how I got pranked, and they'll actually be admitting me after all. Or an invitation to some secret club for people who were too good for Gladstone.

You know, for somebody who grew up in Disappointmentsburg, Pennsylvania, the pain still sucks.

Mom gives me a hug. "It's okay. There'll be other art programs."

"Yeah, those chumps don't know what they're missing," Nathan says.

Even Dad gruffly nods.

I lost a dream today. But the thing about not getting into Gladstone: someone else at Evergreen must have gotten in.

When it's finally time to go to school, Mom bids me and Nathan good-bye as bus 19 pulls up. "Love you," she says to me.

I give her a hug. "Love you too."

Nathan resists the hug at first, like he does every morning, but he grumbles, "Love you, too" before he walks with me to the bus stop, waving back at Mom.

It's unusual to ride the bus with Nathan—normally he carpools with Marcellus—so I don't expect him to sit with me, but he does. "Your engineering class starts next week," I say.

"Yeah."

"Are you nervous?"

Nathan laughs. "Me? I'm never nervous." Which we both know is a lie.

We ride in silence for most of the slow-moving trip. Until Nathan whispers, "How am I doing?"

"Huh?"

"Been thinking about it, that's all. How am I . . . doing?"

Don't ever become like Dad. Use your smarts for good. Don't let darkness take you over. Even if Dad changes, don't be like how he was. That's my wish.

I smile. "You're doing great."

Nathan smiles back. He musses my hair, and I don't flinch from his touch.

The thing about being the subject of rumors is eventually newer, more interesting rumors will surge up and take your place, and you can go back to being in the background. Some eighth graders graffiti'd parts of a bathroom, and Principal Dorset's toupee may or may not have come off in the hall, and the new vending machine outside Miss Richter's room is already broken. Still, it seems like whenever Odin and I walk somewhere together, people stare, but they're not always bad stares. Whether they're stares of amusement, curiosity, or support, I can't tell. And I still get called *Galan* and shoved every now and then, but ever since the enthigacs, it's been less of a big deal.

I think that's what I always wanted. For it not to be a big deal.

First things first: the first thing I do in homeroom is walk up to Odin and say, "Congrats," with a big smile on my face.

He looks up from his book and says, "Wait. You didn't—"

"Oh geez. Neither of us—"

He cracks up, and I crack up. I wonder if anyone got in at all from Evergreen. Either way, it's nice to know I still have plenty of room for improvement, I guess.

"I was happy for you," Odin says. "For your success."

"I was happy for you too. Then again, I'm always pretty happy for you."

Odin rolls his eyes. I give him a playful shove, and he smiles.

Next to me, Connor is talking quietly with Sheila. Connor and I haven't spoken since the dance. It's taken every bit of willpower I possess not to apologize up and down for what I did, but if I did that, it would undermine the enthigac. Maybe I'll never speak to Connor Garcia again, never get a big smile directed at me—

"Hey, Alan."

Okay, scratch that. What is this, "Everyone Talk to Alan Day"?

Sheila gives Connor a little push. He says, "Truce?"

"I didn't know we were fighting," I say.

"I was fighting you, I guess. It really sucked what you did to me at the dance, you know."

"I had to do it. Ron—"

"I get it, I get it. It won't happen again."

Sheila smirks. "It better not."

Connor extends a fist. I bump it with my own. "You're a great guy, Alan," he says. "Even if you are too nice." He smiles. Not a big smile, but I'll take it.

On my other side, Odin shakes his head with a soft smile, flipping through the pages of a new book.

"Excuse me?"

Connor, Odin, and I look up and there's a girl standing over my desk. I don't recognize her. "Hi," I say.

"Can I talk to you . . . in the hall?"

Me and Odin give each other looks. "Sure," I say slowly.

The girl follows me into the bustling hallway. We stand next to the new vending machine outside Miss Richter's room, full of candy and chips but no way to reach them (. . . supposedly). "I'm Laura," she says.

"Alan," I say, still unsure what this is about.

"I know," Laura says. "I'm . . . a lesbian."

Oh. Oh wow.

"I came out yesterday. It's been weird. And scary. I guess you know all about that, huh?"

"Y-Yeah."

A few kids in the hall slow down and watch our conversation. Laura rubs her arms together. "You really . . . you inspired me. I never thought I could do it, but watching you handle everything you had to deal with was . . . wow."

My face flushes. "It's hard," I say.

"Yeah."

"But I guess—I guess it gets easier the more you do it. You know what a good friend said to me once?"

"What?"

"He said, *I'd rather have a hard time being myself than an easy time being somebody else.*"

"Whoa."

"Yeah. You're being yourself, and that's what matters."

Laura gives me a faint smile. "Thank you." She pauses. "For everything." She walks off down the hall.

In a daze, I come back to homeroom. After a few

moments of replaying that conversation in my head, I realize what happened.

I changed the world.

I actually changed the world.

I close my eyes and let the waves of change wash over me, visualize the crossroads before me, blaze my own path forward, set the sky on fire, transform everything into art. Life itself is my canvas.

Life itself is my cretpoj.

In the pool locker room, Ron walks by and doesn't acknowledge me, like he's done every day for the past two weeks. There haven't been any more explosions. No more threats. No more punches. I don't know if that will stay the same forever, or if one wrong word or glance would send him back over the edge. But for now, at least, there's peace.

As Ron lingers by the exit to the pool, Marcellus comes up behind me. "You think he's a changed person?"

"He hasn't said anything in two weeks."

"That isn't what I asked."

I think hard. "People don't change overnight. It takes time. You've just got to have faith they'll stay on the right path."

Marcellus walks in front of me. He smiles. "You've

got enough faith for everyone."

I nod. "I guess I do."

Right when I'm about to leave the locker room, I look up, and Ron is standing with his back to me, facing out into the pool, blocking the way.

Silence. He doesn't move. I can't see his face, can't visualize what he's thinking. I don't want to say anything to break the stillness, though I could say how I realized there's no such thing as a "real man," how there are only people who are good and kind and work hard to be their best, and how I hope maybe he realizes that too now. I could say that to him, but I don't. Instead I wait for him to make the first move.

He turns around. We stare at each other.

Very slowly, he gives me a faint, blink-and-you'd-miss-it nod.

I nod back.

He walks into the pool area, feet plopping along the damp tiles.

I could've said all those things about what it takes to be a real man.

But I guess I didn't need to.

If personal change is like vomiting, Ron just threw up last night's dinner. Maybe all the bile that compelled him to give kids black eyes or to hate gay people got flushed down the toilet. Maybe it's going to be replaced with change, warm and bright and happy. Maybe this is the beginning of a new Ron McCaughlin.

For now though, I'll settle for a nod.

I prepare to follow Ron out into the bleachers, but I'm stopped again by someone else: "Alan."

I walk back to Odin's locker and Odin's sitting there. In a bathing suit.

"You're swimming?" I ask.

"I got over my chlorine allergy," he says, but he doesn't sound too happy about it. He stands up and—

Oh. Oh wow.

His stomach is covered in scars. I can't tell what they are—burn marks? Stab wounds? Something even worse? He holds his hands protectively over his body. "I know my dad told you what happened," he says.

"Not much," I say.

He points to himself. "This is all you need to know."

I don't say anything. I can't say he looks fine, and I can't say nobody will notice. But I can say, "It doesn't matter."

"Yeah?"

"Yeah. It doesn't matter what you look like, and it doesn't matter what they think. All that matters is who you are. You're Odin Thompson, and you'll still be Odin Thompson in the pool and in the locker room and on the bus and in science class and on the moon, and that's great, because Odin Thompson has a good soul, and he shouldn't mind showing it off—"

Odin's mouth silences my words. He pulls back quickly, smiles, and says, "You know something, Corn Beef? You're okay."

I feel my cheeks flush. I smile. "You're okay too. Come on. Let's go for a swim."

"—so then the yodeling sailor says, 'That ain't your baby, it's my cow!'" Zack pounds his fist on the Unstable Table in a fit of laughter so loud people from six tables down turn their heads.

"I've been thinking," Madison says. "Now that I finally told my parents how I felt about the fitness club."

"You did?" I ask.

"Whoa," Zack says. "What did you say? And what did they say?"

Madison sips his bottled water through a straw. "I told them I was tired of stressing out over my appearance. They eventually agreed that perhaps their 'comprehensive fitness program' was doing me more harm than good. They said I could stop as long as I joined a school club."

"That shouldn't be hard," I say. "There's lots of those."

"Join the chess club!" Zack says. "Ooh, or how about the model airplane club! Or the health and fitness club!

Actually, wait, scratch that last one."

I smile at Madison. "You did great by standing up to them."

He smiles back. "Yes. They were still unhappy with me over Meredith too, so I'm impressed they actually listened."

"Do you two still talk?" Zack asks.

Madison nods. "She's a nice girl. But we're better as friends." He whispers to me, "What about you and Odin, hmm?"

Zack asks loudly, "Yeah, what about you and Odin?"

I turn red. "Ask him yourself." I gesture two seats down, at the other end of the normally empty Unstable Table, where Odin sits, flipping through a book. He didn't want to mess with the group dynamic, but I told him there was no way he was sitting alone anymore. This was a compromise.

"Hey, Odin!" Zack yells. "What about—"

"Ask Alan," Odin says without looking up.

Zack grins. "You two are so cute. Hey, so I'm going out with my mom and Theo tonight for dinner. What should I wear?"

"Clothes," I say.

"Done," Zack says. "Whew, that was easy."

"You know something?" I ask. "I'm glad you guys are my friends."

"Hear, hear," Madison says.

"Now and forever and always," Zack says.

Madison, Zack, and I put our thumbs in the middle of the Unstable Table. We're losers. And we're winners too. Never forget that.

At my desk in my bedroom I toil away at my next painting. No Odin on line art this time—this one's all me. Of course, it's not all me at all, really.

It's a zoomed-out group shot. At the far left is Odin, arms crossed, looking sullen, but with a half smirk. Next to him is Madison, shorter than Odin by a lot, adjusting his collar with a confident smile. On the right is Zack, waving goofily up through the canvas (his hair was a lot of fun to draw). And in the center is me, seated, looking up at my friends, a look of pure bliss filling my face. Both my thumbs are raised sky high.

Four people who can't be put into boxes, four people who are complicated—more complicated than you'd think. Four people who are made up of good and bad parts. Four people who are and aren't everything you've seen. Four people who exist.

Four people who've changed. Who never stop changing.

That's only four people. Makes you wonder what the rest of the world is up to.

At 16 Werther Street, in the place I call home, Nathan

Cole listens to music, clomping around his room pretending to conduct an orchestra; James Cole unwinds in front of the TV, feet propped on the ottoman; and Cindy Cole sits next to him, hands intertwined as they watch a movie. Outside the snow rages on. Talia MacDonald writes a letter to her pen pal in Germany. Connor Garcia builds a snowman with his little sister and lets her ride on his shoulders. Marcellus Mitchell relaxes in his room with a sci-fi novel. Miss Kathleen Richter talks with her sister over the phone, insisting for the hundredth time she's happy single. June Harrison stares at the moon and imagines herself there, looking down at Earth with binoculars. Ron McCaughlin tickles his younger brother, Aaron, chasing him all over the house and collapsing into a pile by the front door, laughing all the while. Odin Thompson plays Scrabble with his dad for family game night. Zack Kimble tries prime rib for the first time and loves it to death. Madison Wilson Truman goes for a walk and, when nobody's looking, makes a snow angel.

And Alan Cole is Alan Cole.

That's all there is to say.

ACKNOWLEDGMENTS

Thank you to Brent Taylor, my agent and biggest fan, who leapt at the chance to work on a sequel to *Alan Cole Is Not a Coward* and supported me the whole way through. I said this in the first book's acknowledgments, but it still holds true—you believe in Alan just as much as I do. Thank you to Uwe Stender for editorial guidance and support. Thank you to the rest of #TeamTriada for cheerleading. Thank you to IMC Literary Agency and Book/lab Literary Agency for finding international homes for Alan and his friends.

Thank you to Ben Rosenthal, my editor at Katherine Tegen Books, for amazing editorial feedback, for bringing out the best parts of this book, and for welcoming my input—you truly made me feel like a valued part of this process. Thank you to Mabel Hsu and the rest of the staff at HarperCollins for all the work and effort you put into making my book something special, and for letting me feel like I mattered. Thank you to Julia Kuo for another stellar cover that parallels the first book's but stands on its own. Thank you to Aurora Parlagreco for excellent design work. Thank you to Katherine Tegen for once again trusting in Alan, and once again trusting in me.

Thank you to the Bux-Mont Critique Group—Wendy Greenley, Tamara C. Gureghian, Melissa McDaniel, Jean Ladden, and Joanne Alburger—for helping mold the manuscript from fledgling ideas into a real live book via solid critiquing skills. I'm so privileged to be in your company.

Thank you to my beta readers and trusted writing buddies Joy McCullough-Carranza and Shanna Rogers, without whose sharp feedback this book would not be nearly as polished. Thank you to the 2015 Pitch Wars Mentees group for your support and community.

Thank you to my trusted sources of inspiration who helped me with ideas: Stephen Kittel, Parag S. Gohel, Alan Huan Chang, Nikolai Zarnick, Ali Floyd, Kira Lemke, and Richie George.

And thank you for inviting me—and Alan—into your world. My world is a little bit brighter every time someone reads my book, and I can only hope yours brightens every time you read it too.